MURDER TIMES TWO

Marlene Baird

ISBN: 0-7596-6499-4

This book is printed on acid free paper.

1stBooks - rev. 12/04/01

With gratitude to
family members and friends without whose support
these, and other, characters
would not have life.

PROLOGUE

1965
The Foothills of the Canadian Rockies

Maryanne Beauchamp pushed sweat-plastered hair back from her forehead and prayed, Dear God, let them want two babies. Then another contraction contorted her body. It was as if a bomb had gone off in her midsection. Surely her skin would pop, spitting muscle and tendon and the two little ones into the cold glare of the delivery room. Piercing pain brought a swirl of delirium, and her husband's face as she'd last seen it—brutal and threatening. She hissed. "Martin, may you burn in hell for this!"

Someone said, "It's always the husband's fault."

Maryanne turned to glare into a pair of flat eyes. "What did you say?" she demanded.

"Nothing. Now concentrate on your breathing. It won't be long."

Maryanne sank back against wet sheets, gulping air. What did this stupid nurse know about a man like Martin?

Thank God, Beverly and Gerald McCallister had agreed months ago to adopt the baby Martin refused to acknowledge. When Maryanne learned that she was carrying twins she didn't dare tell the McCallisters for fear they would change their minds. Surely, once they saw the babies, they would take them both. Take both her little ones to safety.

She felt a giant's hands twist her body as if it were a wash cloth. The pain made her eyes roll upwards and the lids flicker, and she groaned as her two sons pushed toward birth.

Marlene Baird

ONE

Roger Bollinger stood inside the sales office, shoulders slumped, hands in pockets—a long-practiced pose that belied the constant churning in his gut. Winter had the city by the throat, and he stared through owlish glasses at a landscape as bleak as his own prospects. Cold radiated from the plate glass window, chilling his face. Near the street, a gaudy purple and yellow sign swung in the wind. It read, *Al's Good Car Deals*, and no matter how you took it—good cars or good deals—it was pretty much a lie. Roger ran one hand through thick, dark hair that curved into his neck. Pathetic, that this was the best place he'd ever worked, maybe the best place he ever would work. Not exactly where he'd hoped to be at thirty-five years of age. Still, it was a long way from his homeless skittering as a young teenager and further yet from his crippling childhood.

As traffic piled at the stoplight on the corner, a Toyota pickup skidded on the icy street, lightly tapping the rear of a pale green Chevy. Neither driver bothered to get out. The pickup backed off an inch or so and the two vehicles sat with dozens of others, huffing steam.

The other two salesmen, standing across the room from Roger, seemed to be arguing about something as they waited on the slow-brewing coffee, but Roger was not interested. He rubbed his mustache and returned his hand to his pocket as his mind raced along a dangerous path. At first he hadn't thought of himself as a murderer, but an executioner. People should pay for their crimes. But over the last few months he'd been massaging every detail of the act; before the law it would be considered premeditated, and harshly punished. Echoing his jumbled thoughts, his fingers began to tumble the few coins in his pockets.

Concentrating, he pictured himself finally in the act, and became overwhelmed with a rush of pure satisfaction. His hands relaxed inside his pockets, his breathing became so shallow he felt delirious.

Henry's voice, which rumbled from the depths of a huge belly, startled him. "Roger, coffee's ready."

Roger blinked. "In a minute."

A band of jagged icicles broke free from the bottom of Al's hideous sign with a sharp, cracking noise, and plunged into the snow bank below. The city had been under glacial siege since November— four months of bone-aching cold. Not for the first time, Roger wished he'd been born in L.A. or Florida. Anywhere in the States would be better than this city, its tentacles reaching ever westward toward the Canadian Rockies, as if the cold-faced mountains were preferable to the prairie's sweeping winds.

The car lot was carved out of the side of a hill. In the valley, beyond the ugly strip malls and clusters of small businesses, Roger could see the city's sharp skyline. Spindly, glass-faced skyscrapers poked into a snow-clogged sky, but Roger was not impressed.

He knew that the higher the building, the longer the shadow, and he was too familiar with their dark alleys lined with cold brick, urine and danger.

He had run away from home at sixteen, sure that nothing in the outside world could match the misery of life with his father. Too soon his nights were spent hunched in the recessed doorways of apartment buildings.

On one such night, a frigid wind moved debris along the sidewalk, swirling it under his legs. His stomach cramping from hunger, he pulled the collar of an ill-fitting coat up over his ears. He rubbed at his right shoulder, still aching so long after the baseball bat had almost shattered it. That last brawl had been terrible; he thought his father might actually kill him. Approaching footsteps made him tuck more tightly into the shadow for fear of the police. But the feet that stopped in front of him were in expensive brown loafers. Roger looked up. The glow from the apartment's interior light showed him the face of a middle-aged man. An odd smile played at the man's lips as he leaned down and pushed a fifty dollar bill in Roger's face. For a moment Roger didn't understand. When he grasped that the man wanted sex, Roger leaped from his crouch, pushed the man off balance and kicked him hard in the groin. The man screamed in pain and fell against the building, the money floating away. Roger followed the fluttering bill, scooped it up and ran. That was, by far, the easiest fifty he ever earned.

During his early jobs he came to know the working end of restaurants very well, especially those the city's inspectors seemed to ignore. Steam sank into peeling walls, where bugs drank. Garbage piled, ripening. But these were the owners who did not ask

5

too many questions of a young man. Roger moved from job to job, flophouse to dingy apartment, always in fear that his father might find him. He changed his last name and dyed his hair to avoid recapture. Not until he was eighteen or nineteen did he realize, with a jolt, that no one was searching for him because no one cared where he was. That day he learned the full depth of abandonment; it was better to be sought by a madman than not to be sought at all.

Recalling the genesis of the loneliness that had defined his life ever since, Roger shifted his feet as if the memory had put him off balance. Suddenly, a shaft of sunlight pierced the morning cloud cover, and one of the city's highrises lit up like a torch. Roger wondered if that was, perhaps, McCallister Plaza.

"Roger, what the hell," Henry called again, "you gonna stand there all damn day?"

He started toward the coffee pot.

Henry folded the newspaper in half and slapped it with the back of his hand. "You guys see this one? The jerk who shot his old lady 'cause she spent his beer money?"

"Jesus, Henry," Richard said, "You're a ghoul. Do you pay any attention to real news?"

Henry grunted amiably. "Don't get your shorts in a knot. I like crime stuff. Human nature, you know? Anybody could kill under the right circumstances, eh?"

Roger's hand trembled as he held his stained cup under the spigot.

"Anyway what's so interesting about *real* news?" Henry continued. "Politics? Look at this McCallister guy."

McCallister? Roger stopped breathing to listen more intently as Henry continued.

"He'll probably get the nomination this afternoon, but shit, he married the boss's daughter. Tough duty."

Roger tried to walk casually towards the men but his knees didn't cooperate, and the coffee rippled in his cup as he approached Henry. "What's that? About McCallister?"

Richard's more reasonable voice answered. "You know. That new party, Majority Party they call themselves, is picking their national leader today. Might be him. Whether he married right or not, I like the guy. Seems sincere."

Henry, always ready to argue, took him on. "Well, I can't stand these silver spooners pretending they know anything about the rest of us. I bet he never ever missed a meal, let alone a paycheck."

"Hey," Richard said, "he's done a good a job with that engineering firm. At least he works for a living— he's not another lawyer."

As they sparred, Roger looked from man to man, seeing lips moving, but hearing almost nothing. McCallister getting the party nomination? Surely not. Roger's head began to swim. He put the coffee cup on the nearest desk, slopping some over, and grabbed his coat from the rack.

"You guys finished with the paper?" he asked.

Henry re-folded it and handed it over. Roger clutched it to his chest as he opened the door and braced himself against the cold. His faded red

Mustang coughed and sputtered as he urged it onto the street.

Roger panted as he ran up the stairway to the second floor of the poorly renovated hotel. For once, he was unaware of the century of smells permeating worn carpets and flaking wallpaper. Once inside his tiny apartment, before he even removed his coat, he scanned the article on Daniel McCallister. The reporter confirmed Richard's high opinion of the young politician.

"Shit!" Roger shouted, the word loud in the small room.

His hands clenched, crushing the paper. He began to tear it into pieces, but that wouldn't destroy it fast enough. He pulled out the offending page, balled it into a tight wad and threw it across the room. If McCallister got the nomination that would be the last straw. Roger stripped off his coat and slammed it on the couch. A small, yellow and orange cat jumped out from behind a cushion and fled to the narrow space between the fridge and the wall.

A year ago, on an impulse, Roger had picked Mangy up outside a convenience store. Her matted coat and thin frame suggested to Roger that they both needed company. In fact, the cat existed very well on food alone and, in spite of Roger's efforts, their relationship had not blossomed. But still Roger courted her; if he could win her, he would have one friend.

Roger kneeled and scratched at the floor.

"I'm sorry I scared you. Come on out."

Mangy fixed him with a flat stare.

"Things are going to happen, cat. I'm almost ready."

Her silence goaded him. "Soon. You'll see."

He stood, and with his hands on the back of his waist, stretched, looking around. The entire apartment could be taken in with one turn of his body. He took pride in his neatness. The bed—in an alcove in the living room—was made as tightly as any military bunk. Even his pain killers and glass of water were lined up just so on the coffee table, like a little army at the ready. The scrapbook sat dead center on the table, with his mother's old diary positioned perfectly on top of that. The TV guide had its own place on top of the set. He found precision necessary, calming.

He wandered into the bathroom and checked his hairline in the mirror. The light roots were just beginning to show. There was no real need to re-color for a week or so, but he retrieved a box of hair dye from a drawer and pulled a grayish towel with dark splotches from under the sink. Draping it over his shoulders, he applied dark brown color with gloved fingers, then carefully applied the color to his eyebrows. Roger realized he was casting about for activities, anything to keep him from thinking about Daniel McCallister.

After dinner Roger sat down on the couch and flicked on the TV. He unconsciously held his breath as the screen flickered teasingly, then faded, then finally burped into service. The dying television set was only one reason he needed to sell a car very soon.

Hoping to lure her close, he put Mangy's dish in his lap. Mangy crept to his feet, looking up. Roger dipped his finger into the food and held it down for her to smell. She licked his finger then jumped to the arm of the sofa. Roger sat very still as she

9

nudged gingerly onto his lap. She took one halting bite, looked up at him, then settled down, gulping hungrily.

Roger changed the channel to watch the blonde anchor he liked. He couldn't imagine her actually going out and getting any news, but she did a nice job of delivery. While he concentrated on her perfectly glossed lips, the words she spoke made him jerk to attention.

"The infant Majority Party has found its legs right here in Alberta. Just an hour ago, local businessman Daniel McCallister was chosen to head the party in its quest for national recognition."

Roger bolted from the sofa. Mangy's dish flew and her food splattered on the coffee table as she skittered away.

Roger threw his hands in the air and screamed obscenities at the ceiling.

As the woman spoke, McCallister's handsome face appeared in a split-screen box in the upper right-hand corner. Roger despised the politician's full, wide smile and the easy confidence in his eyes.

"Daniel McCallister," the blonde continued, "has been a prominent citizen—"

Roger shouted at her. "Shut up."

Roger's blood pumped furiously and he had a glimpse of his fate just before the migraine smacked him with a hammer blow. He moaned and put his hands to his face. With feather-light fingers he gently caressed his forehead and temples. Easy, easy. But he knew there was no stopping it. He slowly leaned over the coffee table. With eyes squinting against the stabbing pain he groped for his pills. He swallowed four of them and sat down, leaning gently back into the cushion. His hand fell on the remote and he turned off the TV before the worst of the headache halted all activity.

He sat, willing his body not to move. Over several hours, in minuscule increments, the pain eased. He drifted in and out of sleep. When the worst seemed to be over, and testing each movement for painful consequences, he slowly got up and rinsed his face with cool water. Then he cleaned up what scattered cat food Mangy had missed.

He wiped at the scrapbook with a damp cloth, but an oily spot now permanently marked its surface. Sitting on the edge of the couch he slowly opened the book. The pages were dog-eared from wear. Its familiar contents recounted what Roger considered Daniel McCallister's greased slide through life.

Filling the scrap book had been easy. Gerald McCallister, Daniel's father, had been mayor of the city for three terms. For years the family appeared in the newspaper regularly. The first clipping showed Daniel at age seventeen, standing proudly behind his father as the senior McCallister cut a wide ribbon. Daniel had learned to smile from his father. The phoniness made Roger want to vomit. Another picture was of Daniel's mother at a fundraiser for disadvantaged children, her own robust son at her side. Roger now regretted the angry pen marks criss-crossing the mother's face. In a fit, he'd tried to obliterate her smile, but now he wished he could study the face of the woman who might have saved him.

Roger moved along a half-dozen pages. A newspaper photo of a beautiful young woman on horseback brought a hint of a smile to his lips— Rosie Jones, a local girl who had made good on the rodeo circuit, until her greed caught up to her. The caption read, "Rodeo Champion Forfeits Title." The reporters had been kind to Rosie, calling disqualification for cheating a forfeit. But who could deny Rosie? She was gorgeous and tough. He'd learned that he would have to behave himself with a woman like Rosie—she could stand up for herself, unlike the silly girls he'd met before her. But, not knowing of Rosie's gumption and ambition when they met, he'd blown his first chance with her. Since then, he'd found her a couple of times, but whenever he made contact she rebuffed him. He'd lost touch now, had no idea where she might be. Saddened, Roger closed the book and set it precisely in the center of the coffee table.

Picking up the diary to place it on top, he couldn't keep himself from fanning the pages. Most of his mother's entries were accounts of terrible, terrible times, but he'd read them all so often they'd become a litany too familiar to evoke any strong emotion. There were only two short passages that affected him now. One calmed him, and the other opened raw wounds. He wished she'd never put McCallister's name in the book. The reference had brought him nothing but dashed hope and desolation.

With effort, Roger dismissed that thought and turned to a dog-eared page. His mother's awkward handwriting, now as familiar as his own, granted him a moment's peace.

Roger turned four today. He's a blonde angel, the only thing that saves me.

Roger traced over the lines with his finger, then gently replaced the diary on top of the scrapbook. He flicked on the TV to watch the late news.

On screen, Daniel McCallister again, in an interview. Roger had no physical energy left with which to protest. The Mini-cam had caught McCallister in front of the building that bore his name, McCallister Plaza. Probably caught was the wrong word, Roger thought. More likely it was planned—where better to be seen than in front of that flashy entry?

A young female reporter, clearly affected by McCallister's good looks, asked a non-question. "Mr. McCallister, you are the youngest man ever to head a contending political party in this country." She shoved the microphone at him for an answer.

McCallister smiled easily, ignoring her remark about his age. "The Majority Party is more than a contender. We're going into the ring with confidence based on solid reasoning and grass-roots support. We have a message and a promise that every citizen can connect with."

The reporter began to pull the microphone back, but McCallister touched her arm, at the same time engaging the camera's eye. "I'd like to invite the wonderful people who have supported me, and all the local Majority Party membership, to join us in a rally tomorrow night at the Convention Center." The reporter started to close out the interview when McCallister spoke again. "Eight o'clock!" he said, giving an enthusiastic thumbs up.

Roger returned the gesture with one of his own. He slumped back into the couch, his fingers tugging at a loose thread as he concentrated. There's got to be a way to stop him. There's got to be a way. Suddenly he sat up straight and grabbed the diary. A smile played at his lips as he realized that, unwittingly, his mother had given him the ammunition he needed.

13

Stroking the softened cover and daydreaming about his success, Roger watched the televised weather report with scant attention until the Mini-cam followed a newly plowed cul-de-sac. Continuous snow piles, at least four feet high, lined the sides of the road. Roger's senses quickened as he saw himself as a youngster sliding down very similar snowbanks. Then he was stunned to see, in the background, the old Ajax Warehouse. This dilapidated building, situated only a couple of hundred yards from his childhood home, had been his sanctuary more than once. He could still smell its labyrinth of dusty cupboards, hear its squeaking passageways, and feel the mystery of dark corners where he hid from his father. But there was one night he remembered most clearly—the night after his eighth birthday.

His mother had made a three-layer cake, the biggest ever. Outside, the first winter storm slammed ice particles against rattling windows. Roger put his hands over his ears to keep out the wind's shrieking hiss and wondered if his father might be swept away in the blizzard. The thought did not disturb him.

His father did not come home for dinner, even though it had been delayed more than an hour. Roger's mother cleaned up the dishes, then began wiping places that weren't dirty. Then she wrapped herself in a thick sweater and went out to the enclosed porch for a cigarette.

"Mom, put on your coat," he had called.

She turned, took a long drag and stubbed out the cigarette. "Your father must have had to work late," she said, stepping back inside. "We might as well go ahead and have the cake."

The next day Roger's father wasn't late, and the three of them sat down to dinner together. Roger expected their usual silent meal, with no conversation, until he noticed that his mother had put on all her makeup. Her hair was piled on top of her head and she wore her flowery dress. Roger's insides contracted; anything out of the ordinary was cause for alarm. He caught her smiling shyly across the table at his father and was relieved when his father ignored her and slurped away at his soup. Roger turned his eyes down to his own bowl.

"Martin," his mother said, "I'm very proud of you, getting that raise."

"Hmph," he said.

The boy's eyes darted from one parent to the other. Usually when his mother started a conversation things did not go well.

She still smiled, but her voice reminded Roger of the scraping of a violin. "With the extra, do you think we might get him a new bed?" On the 'him' she nodded toward Roger. "On credit, only a few dollars a month."

Roger swallowed a lump of fear. Talk about money was the worst kind. His ears started to pound.

His father carefully laid the heavy soup spoon on the table. He sat very still for a moment, dark eyes focused on Roger. "You don't need a new bed, *do* you, son?"

Roger shook his head vigorously.

"Martin, he doesn't know," his mother argued. "That mattress has lumps. It's bad for his back."

Abruptly, his father pushed back from the table, which jiggled on shaky legs. Roger grabbed at his soup bowl with both hands as it threatened to spill. His father leaned close to him.

"Does your back hurt?" The tone of his voice allowed only one answer. He shook his head again.

"See?" his father said. "You worry for nothing."

Roger's teeth clenched as his mother's voice rose. "For goodness' sake, Martin, would you expect him to contradict you?"

The boy froze, hands on the rim of his soup bowl, as his father leaned even closer to him. Hot breath moved over Roger's ear.

"Would you lie to me? Would you?"

Roger knew it was time he gave a firm answer but his voice was locked away.

"Answer me!" his father shouted, shoving at the back of the boy's chair. As the chair tipped, Roger released his bowl and grabbed the table for support. The hot soup slopped across the slick surface, streaming onto his father's lap.

"Damn you," the man yelled, jumping up. He swiped at Roger with a meaty hand, grazing his cheek.

The boy heard a cry, a scraping chair, and suddenly his mother stood between them, trying to grab at his father's hands.

"Stay out of this," his father warned.

They struggled above him for only a moment until the man's strength overcame her. She fell backwards on top of Roger, both of them crashing to the floor. They scrambled beneath the table, trying to untangle from one another and from the toppled chair.

His mother shouted at Roger. "Get out of here." She pushed him toward the door. "Get out!"

He scurried on all fours to the doorway and stood. He turned to see his father shove the table away and kick at his mother.

Finally, his voice broke free in a childish scream. "Stop it! Stop it, or I'll kill you!"

The words hung in the air. The sudden silence was thick, and deep enough to drown in. His mother stared up at Roger with stark fear in her eyes. He felt dizzy. No one breathed.

Then his father scowled, his voice going quiet. "You little bastard," he hissed, lunging at the boy.

His mother kicked out with a foot, knocking him off balance. "Run!" she shouted to her son. "Run!"

Roger raced out the back door and across the vacant field, the echo of his father's rage lapping at his heels. Yesterday's wind had crusted the three-inch deep snow and Roger felt his ankles being scraped by the crystals where his socks had pulled down. Within a few minutes he reached the door of the abandoned warehouse, his refuge. He clattered over the metal 'Ajax Storage' sign that had long since fallen from its rusted hinges. He flung himself inside and looked back through a broken window. His father had not followed him, but he knew he would. He plunged into the dim recesses of the building, searching for a new hiding place.

Snow had swept in and banked in places, cutting off some of his secret corners. His desperate eyes found a fine line that cross-cut the heavy planks. He dropped to his knees and dug feverishly at the sliced area with narrow fingers, lifting out a wooden square about two feet by two feet. A trap door opened into an earthen hole, pitch black and smelly. He lowered himself down, grateful when his toes reached bottom.

Roger pulled the door over the opening and sat down in the frozen earth. He strained to hear voices, but could not. Long minutes went by and he began to worry about his mother. At least if he heard his father's boots in the warehouse it would mean he had finished with her.

Finally they came, stalking the building. His father didn't call his name, but the boy could hear snuffly breathing like that from a huge animal. The boots came in his direction. They stopped right on top of him and he waited for his father's weight to collapse the little door downward. Holding his breath, Roger hunched down further, hands over his head. Then the steps moved on.

Forever he sat in the darkness. When his body became so cramped and cold that he could no longer stand it, he pushed the trap door open a crack and heard his mother calling him. He shoved the door upward, got out and carefully replaced it, scanning the darkness for a body lurking in wait. Sensing he was alone, he went to the window and saw his mother's form outlined against the lights of the house, running toward him.

He scrambled from the building and threw himself against her, his body heaving with sobs.

She smoothed his hair and comforted him. "He won't ever hurt you, he won't ever hurt you," she kept repeating. "He promised me."

When they got to the house where he could see her face and her arms, he knew the terrible price she had paid for that promise.

Roger blinked, surprised to find himself curled on the sofa, legs tucked close, as though he were still in that dank hole. The TV was broadcasting a black-and-white movie. Suddenly it occurred to Roger that his father might not still be in that house. Martin Beauchamp might already be dead. He shucked off the possibility. He'd pictured himself so often, entering the house and finding his father, that it simply had to happen that way. Still, why had he waited so long? What if he'd lost his chance?

Roger hadn't thought of God in years, but he offered up a shallow prayer now: that his father would still be there. Surely the Almighty owed him something.

TWO

Seeing her boss's door ajar, Rosie Jones peeked in. She'd long ago traded in her tooled cowboy boots for knee-high suede, and her fringed rodeo outfits for cashmere and wool. Daniel McCallister sat deep in thought, his chair pointing him at the floor-to-ceiling window. He did not move. She licked her lips, gave a quick knock on the open door, and entered. "I'm just heading out. Have you got a minute?"

Daniel glanced over his shoulder. "One or two. I'm getting a few thoughts together for the rally."

Pulling on leather dress gloves in a rich coffee brown that matched her coat, she gave him a broad grin. "I don't know about you, but I can't stop smiling since the nomination."

Daniel grinned at her, then chuckled, swiveling his chair to face her directly. "I can hardly believe it either. When I was young I never, ever, dreamed of accomplishing anything like this. It's just fabulous; everything anyone could ask for."

"Well, people don't get ahead because of their good looks, you know. You deserve it."

Daniel, seeming shy of the compliment, turned back to business. "Is everything set at the Convention Center?"

"I'm on my way over there now to give things a last minute check." Rosie stepped further into his office. "You were terrific in those impromptu interviews yesterday. I taped both newscasts in case you want them."

"Sylvia missed them; she'll be glad to have the chance to see them."

Rosie's smile dropped a notch. She hadn't stopped in to remind him of his beautiful wife.

"Should I order a limo to pick you up at the house?"

Daniel gave her a sideways grin that made her stomach clutch. "Always thinking of my image aren't you? No, not tonight. It might look better if we drove. We're not elected yet."

"We will be." Rosie hitched her alligator handbag over her forearm. "Well, I'm on my way. See you when, about seven-thirty?"

"I'll try to be early to get the feel of the place."

"Knock 'em dead." She gave him a broad wink as she closed the door behind her.

Daniel smiled. Rosie had a knack for making him feel good about himself. He'd hired her, young and inexperienced, because at the time he believed his chances of winning the nomination were slim. But he'd surprised himself, with no small amount of credit due to Rosie's efforts. She had a feel for public relations that was missing in his own makeup.

Moving from industry to politics had proved to be a giant shift. In business he controlled his own destiny; in politics public opinion was everything—unnerving. Winning the nomination was a great accomplishment, but the real work lay ahead. The

21

next two years, preparing for the general election, would be hectic and exciting ones.

He returned to the notes in front of him and by six-fifteen he felt he had his thoughts in order. He pulled on his jacket and put the papers in his briefcase. Sylvia would be anxious if he didn't get home with plenty of time to shower and change. As he moved around his desk the phone rang. His impulse was to leave it, but an ingrained sense of responsibility made him pick it up.

Barry Levy, his attorney, sounded upset. "I need to talk to you," he said. "In person."

"Look, Barry, can't this wait until tomorrow? I've got to be at the Convention Center before eight. I need to get home and pick up Sylvia."

"It's about Sylvia."

"What about her?"

Barry's voice was commanding. "It has to be face-to-face, and completely private. I'll be in the parking lot in ten minutes. Be in your car."

Sylvia McCallister sat on the silk-covered vanity chair, tapping her foot nervously. These two-minute waits were interminable. She watched the second hand on her watch. Fifty-eight, fifty-nine, sixty. She looked at the strip in her hand. Nothing. Negative, again. She sighed, repackaged the paraphernalia and took it out to the large garbage can in the garage. No need for Danny to be reminded of another failure. He didn't know how often she checked, anxious to be able to give him the good news.

Sylvia would welcome a baby, but did not feel as obsessive as Danny about having a child. He wanted three or four. For the first five years of their marriage they'd been careful not to get pregnant, and for the last ten had been just as anxious to start a family. Mother Nature had not responded to their change of heart. The really disturbing by-product of their quest was that lovemaking had become purposeful. No matter how momentarily satisfying, it never seemed complete so long as the desired result evaded them.

Sylvia moved to the massive closet and fingered a dozen possible outfits for this, the most important night so far in Danny's new career. She chose a simple blue silk dress. She thought about the diamond necklace Danny had just given her for their anniversary. It would be a nice gesture to wear it, but she knew that would be too flashy for her first major public appearance. She clipped on a conservative gold rope.

The chiming of the hall clock reminded her that they were in danger of being late for the rally. Just as she picked up the phone to call the office she heard Danny's car pull into the driveway, followed by a screech of brakes. The front door slammed and Danny ran up the steps. He burst into the bedroom, stripping his jacket and shirt.

She reached to take the clothes from him. "Hi, darling. We're really pushing it."

She held her cheek up for a kiss but he rushed past her, giving her a fierce scowl.

"Danny?" she asked, "what's the matter?" She followed him into the bathroom.

He dashed water under his armpits, grabbed a towel and turned toward her. His mouth opened to speak, but no sound came out. His eyes, assessing her, squinted, as if trying to see her more clearly. He shook his head.

Was he sick? She touched his arm. "Danny? What is it?" she demanded.

He moved away from her hand. "I've just had a very enlightening conversation with Barry." He dried himself and rubbed on deodorant. Sylvia waited. His breathing was erratic; she'd never seen him so upset. Barry, their lawyer, could be the source of almost anything.

"Are we being sued?"

A sharp, sarcastic grunt escaped her husband's chest. "Don't I wish," he sneered. His fingers fumbled awkwardly with the buttons on a clean shirt. She wanted to help, but thought better of it.

"It seems you've been keeping quite a secret. An important secret, and for fifteen bloody years."

Sylvia stared at him, her mouth slightly open.

He began to nod. "Yes, I can see you know exactly what I mean."

Sylvia moved back to the bedroom. She sat on the edge of the bed trying to breathe. Her head fell forward like a ponderous weight, and the back of her neck felt as bare as one waiting for the executioner's blade.

"Danny, I can explain—"

"Not now. We're late." He strode from the bathroom and grabbed his jacket off the bed. He galloped down the stairs and out to the car, leaving her to lock the house.

During the drive she tried to approach him again but he put her off. "Later," he snapped. "I need to get my head in the right place for this damned rally." She could see the muscles in his jaw move as he gritted his teeth.

Roger's Mustang didn't idle well and he groaned as the crawling traffic came to a complete halt. Roger cursed as the engine sputtered and threatened to die. To add to his agony, the long line of cars waiting to enter the Convention Center parking lot meant McCallister's rally was a tremendous success.

The crowd filled the auditorium, overflowing into the lobby. Roger pushed his way forward. There were no chairs set up, everyone stood. As he moved through the throng there was a sudden swell of clapping to his left. Roger turned to see the perfectly groomed head of light-brown hair enter through another door. It shocked him to realize that he had never before seen McCallister in the flesh. He was so familiar with the man's life through the clippings in his scrapbook that he felt they were well acquainted.

"Hey, Buddy, what's your hurry?" a man muttered as Roger elbowed his way forward. Roger ignored him, and the others who complained, and made his way to the front. He squeezed in next to a heavy-set woman who glared at him.

Roger watched McCallister help his wife up the last steps to the stage. She was much better looking than her pictures. Sleek, silvery blonde hair framed wide eyes almost the color of her dress. What must it be like to have a woman with her kind of class at your side?

McCallister put his arm around Sylvia's shoulder as several cameras recorded the moment. Roger saw that their smiles did not reach their eyes—this display of affection was strictly for public consumption. Trouble in paradise? One could hope.

The music stopped and many eyes turned to a redhead testing the microphone, tapping it with long, polished nails. She seemed unaware of her stunning

25

appearance as she concentrated on her task. Satisfied, she motioned to McCallister. Then, with her arms outstretched, she urged the crowd to a welcoming crescendo. McCallister stepped up to the mike amidst a great roar of approval.

But Roger barely heard the clamor. His eyes were still glued to the redhead. Was it possible? He shook his head slowly from side to side, disbelieving his good fortune. He added ten years from the time of the rodeo and realized she would be twenty-six now. Twenty-six, and evidently on McCallister's staff. He nodded to himself. It fit. Rosie always knew how to get what she wanted.

The day he first met her he was working at the fairgrounds. After a spell of bad luck with jobs, he had welcomed two weeks' work as a carnival hand. However, only two days into the job, he found the smell of cotton candy nauseating, and the excited squeals of young girls, as they boarded the rides, had lost their charm. But the long hours kept him out of his rented bedroom and the pay was decent. He strapped two giggly girls into the seat of the Ferris Wheel, stepped back for a last check of all the riders, then engaged the heavy lever that set the ride in motion.

Wiping grime from his forehead with the back of his arm, he looked around for his partner, Jimmy. He stretched his arms overhead trying to release the biting tension between his shoulder blades.

Jimmy finally approached, ambling along in his bow-legged swagger. Jimmy travelled with the midway year-round. Forty years old to Roger's twenty-five, he acted like an older brother, and tried to talk Roger into joining up when they left the city.

Though tempted, Roger knew it wouldn't work—he'd only end up hitching a ride back.

"Okay, Bollinger, you're free," Jimmy said.

Roger was so accustomed to his new last name that his real one, Beauchamp, never entered his head any more. The false ID had cost him a bundle, and since his father had apparently never tried to find him, perhaps it was wasted money. Still, he preferred the extra distance between him and his past.

Jimmy dug into his jeans pocket. "Hey, this little gal I know works in the grandstand. She gave me this infield pass to the rodeo. Want it?"

Roger knew very little about rodeos but he didn't have plans for his two hour break. "Sure. Thanks."

"You going to join up when we break camp tonight?" Jimmy asked.

Roger shook his head. "Naw. But thanks."

Roger threaded his way through the crowded midway: hawkers coaxing him to try rigged games of chance; smells of grilling onions, hot dogs and hamburgers assaulting him; wide-eyed children with sticky fingers, straggling after parents. In ten minutes he entered the grandstand area. It took him some time to locate the tunnel that took him under the race track to the infield. His seat was near the top of the ten rows of bleachers. He soon realized that if you went to the rodeo, this was the place to be. In the awning-covered stands off to his left he spotted two movie stars, and the female rocker who would be performing that night.

Roger looked across the rodeo arena to the main grandstand. Its wide arc stretched along the race track, almost reaching to the first and fourth turns. It rose four levels, the top two encased in glass. He guessed there were more than fifty thousand spectators, a good percentage in cowboy hats.

Behind him, the sun beat down on a moving sea of livestock, penned in a maze of pipe corrals. Orange-shirted stock handlers in black western hats shifted gates, shouted and slapped rumps as they moved the animals, sorting them for the events.

The man sitting beside him held his program in front of Roger and pointed to the event, "Ladies Barrel Racing." Roger had a momentary flash of women with barrels strapped over their shoulders racing around the arena, just before a young woman on horseback charged into his line of vision. The man tensed. "That's my daughter," he said proudly.

The girl urged her horse in a sharp turn around a barrel at the edge of the arena. Their bodies were so tilted into the turn that Roger thought the horse would lose his footing. But he didn't, and they raced toward a second barrel, circled that and then charged for a third. They cut the third and last barrel too close and the woman's leg toppled it. The man groaned. "Five-second penalty," he mumbled. Then he jumped to his feet. "Go Jennie, go girl!"

The young woman rose in her stirrups like a jockey. She lashed the horse, whipping the reins from side to side. The horse scattered the loose dirt wildly as his hooves thundered under his massive body. He seemed to be stretching his neck as they burst through the timing beam and out of the arena.

The crowd applauded politely. The woman's time appeared on an electric scoreboard at the same time as the rodeo announcer said it aloud. "With the penalty, twenty-two point five seconds. Too bad, might have been a winner."

Roger's neighbor slapped his program against his knee. "Shit!" he said.

Roger saw the daughter, still on horseback, move through a staging area where several attractive contestants were gathered. He decided to take a closer look. Moving to the aisle, he descended to ground level. Once among the corrals he perched his skinny butt on a metal railing. A few people glanced at him, but accepted him when they saw the employee ID pinned to his T-shirt.

The dust, churned up by the hooves of nervous animals, almost choked him. Pungent smells attacked his nostrils—people sweat, animal sweat, urine and manure. He cleaned his wire-rimmed glasses with the bottom of his shirt. Damp hair clung to the back of his neck.

As soon as Roger got his first look at Rosie Jones, all the other women paled. He watched her move her horse slowly into line behind another contestant. Long, wavy red hair spilled out from under her hat. She wore a turquoise outfit with silver fringe that dangled over her breasts, catching the sun. Small against the bulk of her horse, she handled the animal with utter confidence and ease. Only her eyes showed a hint of uncertainty as she seemed, furtively, to scan the area, looking for someone. Roger saw her gaze connect with one of the orange-shirted stock boys. The young man tilted his hat in her direction, then left the area. Boyfriend? No. The look was more secretive than affectionate.

Roger looked back at Rosie. She turned slightly in the saddle and their eyes met. He saw a flicker of anxiety. He gave her a broad smile and a wave. She simply laid the reins across the horse's neck and they moved in a slow circle.

29

The rodeo announcer's voice boomed above them. "Now to the climax of this week's events. Coming up, the runoff between our two leaders, Rosie Jones of Calgary and Linda Ainsworth from Bozeman, Montana."

A hefty girl on a large horse moved to the starting gate. Her horse side-stepped abruptly, apparently eager to be moving. She leaned forward and talked into his ear, patting his neck. Roger admired the way she controlled the jittery animal as they moved into place.

The announcer shouted Linda's name. With a well-muscled arm, she smacked the horse's withers with the rein and they burst into the arena. The big chestnut broke through the timing beam with a lunge and raced toward the first barrel. They cut too close to the barrel and it tipped over. The crowd gave a low moan. Now, desperate to make the best possible time, the woman raked his belly with her spurs and whipped him toward the second barrel. They both leaned very low into the turn. The crowd gasped in shock as her saddle slid completely under the horse, throwing Linda headlong into the dirt. The spooked horse spun wildly, hooves grazing her body.

A mounted cowboy raced from the end of the arena to capture the horse. Stretcher bearers moved toward Linda Ainsworth, who was bruised, but conscious, crawling on hands and knees.

Roger turned his eyes to Rosie. She paid no attention to the drama in the arena. She sat calmly mounted, stroking the neck of her horse, eyes downcast, as though mentally readying herself for her run. Though shocked by her indifference, Roger found himself drawn to her self-possession. Was it possible Linda's fall hadn't surprised her? If she had expected the accident—had something to do with it—perhaps that knowledge would give him a little leverage when he asked her for a date that evening.

Now, looking at her up on McCallister's stage, he saw that same intensity of purpose in her face. A gorgeous ally in the enemy camp. What more could he ask?

The bulging arms of the woman next to Roger nudged him as she raised them overhead and clapped loudly. Her eyes were glued to McCallister's face in adoration. Everyone was cheering. McCallister held his arms out, waiting for quiet so he could continue.

"After the worst of crimes, it often seems that those who go to jail are the lucky ones. Just two nights ago, on the newscast, we saw graphic evidence of society's worst nightmare—the drive-by shooting. An innocent child sitting in a high chair, eating her dinner, hit in the head by a random bullet." Several in the crowd moaned in recognition of the story. "There isn't enough punishment anywhere to equal the loss of that child, or to ease the terrible pain of the family." As his voice fell the room went quiet. His eyes flashed to Sylvia. Roger saw the blood drain from her face as McCallister continued. "Any killing is indefensible, but if you lose a child it is especially painful. You lose him or her at that particular age, and you lose him or her at every age thereafter."

McCallister paused, then spoke slowly, almost privately. "I don't have a little girl or boy, yet, but when I do I will truly be able to feel the same fear many of you know every day." Then his chin jutted out. His voice began to rise. He raised his fist, punctuating his words with jabs. "So! Let's join today in a pledge. Whatever it takes, no matter what it takes, we will protect our children, and we will make our homes and streets safe again."

The applause began as a ripple, then built rapidly. He shouted over it. "And starting here, tonight, in this building, we are creating a party platform that will take our message to the entire nation." He stepped back from the microphone with a hearty wave as a tumultuous cheer rose from the floor.

Supporters surged toward the stage to congratulate McCallister. Roger tried to avoid being crushed as he watched Rosie, ever at attention, gauging the reaction of the crowd.

Finally the enthusiasm died, tired from its own effort, and people began to leave. When McCallister and his wife were gone, Roger saw Rosie part the heavy curtains at the back of the stage and step between them. Roger moved slowly, drifting toward the side of the wide stage. He sat on its edge for a moment, then casually swung his legs up. He stood, and without looking back, walked quietly behind the curtain.

He stood still to let his eyes get accustomed to the dark. Rosie was barely visible in the dim, cavernous area; he could distinguish only her body's profile. She sat about forty feet away, on a folding chair, her head resting on its metal back. Her shoes had been kicked off. He heard music. Was she humming? He tilted his head. Yes—a lazy, low, sensuous tune he didn't recognize. She rubbed at one leg with her toe and stretched her hands over her head.

Roger took a step toward her. Rosie stopped, arms frozen above her head. The humming stopped. She apparently wasn't sure which direction the noise had come from. He took another two steps.

Rosie leaped from her chair. She grabbed for her shoes, put them on, stood straight and turned to face him. As he moved closer he could hear her breathing.

"Can I help you?" she said, too loudly.

He admired her spunk. Clearly he'd frightened her, but she stood her ground. He stopped about ten feet from her, hands in his pockets.

"I just wanted to say I'm a great supporter of McCallister's and wanted to wish you well."

"Oh, thank you so much." She sounded relieved, but she took a step backwards. "Thank you for coming tonight. I think it was a great success. He's a wonderful man—"

"Are you his assistant?"

She was moving backwards again. He took a step toward her.

Rosie looked around quickly. "I really need to be going."

A scraping sound made them both turn. The giant curtain was parted in the middle. In the opening they saw the outline of a slim man, backlit by the auditorium lights. "Rosie? You back here?"

Rosie ran to him. "Oh, good, Billy," she said, "I need to talk to you." She linked her arm in his and they disappeared back into the auditorium.

After shaking the thousandth hand stuck in front of him, Daniel broke free from the crowd. As soon as he and Sylvia stepped outside, a uniformed limo driver touched his arm and motioned him toward the car. They climbed in and were swept away in blessed solitude.

Daniel opened the glass partition. "Who called for you?" he asked the driver.

"A Miss Jones, sir. She also asked for someone to take your car home for you. It will be there when you arrive."

"What about the keys?" Daniel said, automatically reaching into his pocket.

"She gave us a key, sir."

Daniel slid the glass closed. Rosie was priceless. He sank back into the seat enjoying a moment of peace until he felt Sylvia's eyes on him. He didn't acknowledge her. There was not enough privacy here for what they had to discuss.

His mind raced with accusations, but when they entered the house and it was time to face the matter, Daniel felt the last ounce of energy drain from his body. "I'm going to bed," he said.

"No, Danny." Sylvia's tone was firm. She draped her coat over a kitchen chair. "We need to talk first. You have to understand. I'll make us some tea. Or coffee?"

He slumped into a chair. "Whatever."

He propped his elbows on the table and rubbed his face with both hands, fingers scrubbing at his eyes. "I can't talk about it," he said.

She sat down opposite him, waiting, forcing him to look at her. "You know I love you more than anything. I always have, and always will."

He didn't want to hear it. His lips closed in a tight line; his eyes blinked in rapid movements.

"I can explain how it happened."

He shook his head at her. Then he straightened and gripped the edges of the table. "Sylvia, what can

34

you possibly say to change the fact that you killed our child?"

He saw her head snap back as though she'd been hit, as her hand flew to her mouth. "Oh, my God," she cried. "Danny, it wasn't like that!"

"What else could it be?" he shouted. His chair toppled as he jumped to his feet and leaned across the table. "Abortion is killing."

She backed further into her chair.

"That's why we can't have any more. Isn't it? What the hell did you do to yourself—to us?" He stared her down until he felt tears in the corners of his eyes. Then he flung himself away and bounded up the stairs, his topcoat flying out behind him.

Daniel paced the guest room for a long time before he could calm down enough to remove his clothes. In the dark sleepless hours, when even the simplest concerns are magnified beyond recognition, his anger at Sylvia flared white hot. Twice he heard her moving about, and had to restrain himself from storming into their bedroom and confronting her anew. It was the immutability of it that ate at him. He was by nature a problem solver, but there was nothing he could do to change this. He threw his pillow across the room in frustration.

Just before dawn, emotionally and physically drained, he sank into a stuporous sleep. In his dreams a young boy, freckled and grinning, ran full tilt toward him. Daniel tucked the football under his arm and faked a move to his right. The boy, not fooled, stayed right on track and threw his body into Daniel with a whoop of victory. They fell to the grass, tangled together, laughing.

Daniel jerked awake, sweating and confused. He lay still, recalling details. The boy in the dream had such a familiar face. Why? Until today Daniel had never even known of the possibility of a son, much less pictured him. Then he moaned aloud and sank back into the sheets. It was Brian's face. The boy in the dream was both the child he'd lost, and Brian, the invisible friend who'd kept him company during his lonely childhood.

THREE

Cathy Tanner rode the elevator to the twentieth floor of McCallister Plaza and stepped out into the elegant reception area that was her domain. She'd worked for McCallister Engineering for only a year, and was naive enough to believe that the surroundings lent prestige to her job. Two walls behind her massive receptionist's desk bore the city's history in dozens of framed black-and-white photographs. She could recite their stories, and often did, for visitors who waited on her boss.

The most historic photo was of a Mounted Police post built where the Bow and Elbow Rivers meet, circa 1875. The rivers' juncture was not far from where she stood at the top of McCallister Plaza, but that wooden fort was a million miles from the sophisticated city it had become. A small contingent of Mounties from the east had set up camp there to halt the whiskey trade with the Indians. In order to feed their railroad crews, opportunists traded liquor to the Indians for buffalo meat—a trade that benefitted only one side.

The settlement grew slowly, drawing mostly on the ranches in the area for commerce. But in 1914 everything changed. In an attempt to locate oil at a small town nearby, drillers tapped a pocket that shot natural gas from the ground with a hiss that ignited the economy. Speculators set up shop in every hotel room. Housewives traded grocery money for risky stocks, and many families went hungry for that effort. But enough solid development took place to put the city on the map. Then, in 1947, with a major oil discovery farther north, the city boomed.

American money and American talent flowed across the border and every major oil company established a foothold. CEO's of Texaco, Standard Oil, British American, Atlantic Richfield and Socony-Mobil were among many others sitting in glossy offices, producing heady payrolls. Investors in smaller drilling and exploration companies became rich. A whole subsidiary industry was established, supplying materials and equipment for the oil fields—from drilling bits to temporary living quarters.

In time the champagne bubbles began to burst, but a cosmopolitan city had been created, with a plethora of millionaires and more cars per capita than any other city in North America.

McCallister Plaza symbolized that prosperity, and Cathy Tanner knew how proud Daniel was of the ingenuity and personal industry it represented. Cathy put her purse on the horseshoe-curved walnut desk and moved to a closet to hang up her coat. The third wall of the reception area bore a huge painting of golden wheat fields under a flawless blue sky. Daniel had told her that was how the family homestead had looked two generations ago, before it became dotted with hard pumping oil derricks.

Daniel's door was closed; apparently he didn't want to be disturbed. But Rosie's was open a crack. Cathy stuck her head in.

"Back from the dentist," she said.

Rosie glanced up from the notes she was making on a yellow legal pad. "How was it?"

"Good. He changed his mind on the root canal. Said we can wait and see."

"Lucky you." Rosie searched her desk for a moment, then handed Cathy two phone messages. "These came for you," she said, barely looking up. It was clear she didn't appreciate having to cover for Cathy, even for a couple of hours. "Please hold my calls until after lunch."

Rosie's office, beside Daniel's, offered the same magnificent view of the mountains, but she seldom noticed. Things had been moving very fast since the nomination. Her main task right now was to organize as many speaking engagements for Daniel as he could fit into his already busy schedule. She had his weekly itinerary on her computer screen, transferring details to a lined pad, when Cathy buzzed her. She couldn't keep the irritation out of her voice.

"Yes?"

"I know you said to hold your calls, Rosie, but this man says it's about the rally last night, and insists that you would want to talk to him."

"Oh, all right." She poked the blinking button on her phone with the eraser end of a pencil and grabbed up the receiver.

"Rosie Jones," she said.

"Hi Rosie. It's Roger."

She dropped the pencil. Surely not.

"Roger who?" she asked, hoping she was wrong.

His voice took on a disappointed tone. "Come on. It's been a while since I called. Two years, actually,

39

give or take a few months, but I know you remember."

Rosie looked to the open door. Her voice dropped. "How did you find me this time?"

"I saw you at McCallister's rally. You still stand out in a crowd." Rosie cringed at the complimentary tone in his voice. "If someone hadn't interrupted us afterwards we could have had a little talk."

It took her a moment, then Rosie's heart leapt. My God, behind the curtain, that was him. She stood up, stretching the phone cord so she could walk over and close her door. It scared her to think he'd been that close and she hadn't recognized him.

She adopted a brave tone. "Well, you're wasting your time, again. How many times do I have to say I'm not interested?"

"Jeez, Rosie. Take it easy. Did I ask for anything? I just want to stay in touch."

"For what? Look, I'm getting a little sick of you hounding me. In fact, I think they call it stalking these days. And it's illegal. I want this relationship, if you can call it that, to end."

His voice was incredulous. "Stalking? Rosie, have I ever threatened you? I just want us to be friends."

He sounded sincere, but the fact that he'd found her again was upsetting. Still, up to now he'd been harmless. Maybe it would be safer to reason with him.

"Roger, listen. I've got the first really great job of my life here. It's my future as far as I'm concerned. In fact, I'll bet you're doing a lot better, too, than you were when we last spoke." He didn't offer anything. "I really wish you well. But my life is totally changed. I've got a lot of responsibility. Heck, I don't

40

even have a social life, and I don't want one right now."

She waited for a second. Nothing. "Roger?"

"Yeah, I'm here." He sounded annoyed. "Can't we just have lunch or something?"

Rosie's mind raced. Better to meet with him and get to know what he's up to? Or would that just encourage him further? She decided on the latter. "I'm truly sorry, Roger. I just don't think it's a good idea."

There was a pause on his end. "Goodbye Rosie."

The hollow finality in his tone gave her the creeps. Work forgotten, Rosie wrapped her arms around her upper body and moved to the window. She concentrated on how he'd looked in the dim light last night, back stage. A mustache dominated his face to the exclusion of his other features. But she had the sense of a lot of dark hair. And sideburns. Yes, full sideburns. For some reason he'd gone to some effort to change his appearance. That was spooky. How long now since they'd first met? Ten years? He was persistent.

She remembered vividly the first time she'd seen him; caught him staring at her at the barrel racing finals. She was sure Roger had seen the stock boy signal her just before Linda Ainsworth's ride. She couldn't imagine that Roger knew of her conspiracy to loosen Linda's saddle, but when he'd asked her out for dinner there was something in his eyes that said he suspected. That's why she'd agreed to the date; she needed to find out what he knew, and if he could be trusted to keep her secret. When, months later, she was stripped of her title, she wondered if an angry Roger could possibly have had anything to do with that.

The night of her victory he'd taken her to a decent place to eat. But no matter where you went in the city during Stampede Week noisy Western bands drowned out conversations. She leaned forward to catch his words.

"You'd have won anyway, you know," he said.

"Anyway?" Rosie tilted her head and studied him. Their eyes locked. His were teasing, knowing.

"Even if that other gal hadn't fallen," he answered smoothly. Then he taunted her. "Does that kind of accident happen often?"

Rosie shrugged. "Equipment problems can happen if you're not careful."

"Ever happen to you?"

"I'm always careful."

He laughed. "I'll bet you are." He raised his beer glass to her. "To good planning."

She smiled at him, letting him have his little victory. He acted as if he knew her, when he knew nothing. She never trusted chance; her years on the family ranch had taught her that. She and her two sisters worked like men. In winter, no matter the temperature, you got hay out to the cattle—with frozen fingers if necessary. In spring you branded every last one of the calves regardless of the effect their bellowing had on your heart. And then the girls slaved with their mother. For a week straight they baked bread and rolls for the giant freezer in the basement so that the next week was free for more important work, like putting up preserves. It was a hard life and it had taught her to cover all the contingencies.

"Where'd you learn to ride like that?"

"I'm a ranch hand," she smirked.

"Really?" His eyebrows shot up; then he realized she was joking. "Oh, you mean your family has a ranch."

Rosie nodded.

"That must be a good life," Roger suggested.

His tone seemed wistful. His own life must be pretty pitiful if he envied her.

The twanging music and crush of bodies suddenly seemed to be closing in on her. Rosie picked up her jacket, ready to leave. "I hate the ranch. Once I leave for college I'm never going back."

When they left the restaurant, Roger insisted they park on the cliffs just above the Stampede Grounds, ostensibly to watch the fireworks display that ended the evening's performance. Every young person in the city knew it as the very best makeout spot in town but Rosie felt confident she could control the situation.

Roger's pickup was old, but immaculate. Clean and shiny outside, spotless inside. He stuck his glasses in the glove compartment and slid closer to her, putting his arm across her shoulders. She let him kiss her, but she kept her lips tightly closed. He sat back and chided her.

"Hey, how about a little enthusiasm?" With his hand behind her neck he pulled her close again and tried to force her mouth open with his tongue. She moved her head from side to side to escape its probing, backing into the corner of the seat. Her right hand slid down behind her, searching for the door handle. Just as she was about to push on it, Roger reached across her with his left hand and jammed down the door lock.

"Hey, don't panic." He released his hold on her neck. "If you don't like that, it's okay."

Rosie tried to read his eyes as he moved toward her again. His arm moved from her shoulders down to her waist and he pulled her tight against him. A flash of fireworks lit up the cab and Rosie's heart jumped. His eyes were half closed, his face full of lust. She put both hands on his chest. "Hey, I'm only sixteen," she said.

"Sure you are," he said, pulling her head back by her hair and burying his lips in her throat. His body moved over her, forcing her to lay back on the seat.

She screamed, kicking at his door. "No, really! I'm only sixteen. Get off me or I promise . . . you'll go to jail."

She felt him go still, trying to control his body. He didn't move for a full minute. She held her breath.

"You shitting me?" he asked.

"No, I swear to God I'll have the cops on you. Let me up."

Slowly he backed off her.

As soon as she was able to sit upright she unlocked the door and jumped out of the truck. As she ran she heard him yell to her to come back, that it would be all right, but she kept on going.

A few years later he entered her life again. He'd spotted her on the street and followed her to the restaurant where she worked. She quit that job to get away from him. When he found her again, just over two years ago, she'd been a contestant in a local beauty pageant. The caption under the group picture said she was a student at the university. He'd paged her on campus, claiming a family emergency, and spoken to her on the phone. Once she left school she'd felt safe again.

Well, he knew where she was now, and she couldn't quit this job and disappear. Last night's rally had gone incredibly well; she'd found a note from Daniel on her desk early this morning, congratulating her. Rosie never doubted Daniel would one day be the most powerful man in the country, and she was determined to be at his side. No one would ever connect her with the sixteen-year-old rodeo rider who had been disgraced. No one but Roger.

The sound of a knock on her door spun her around.

The door opened and Cathy stuck her head in. "Ready to go?" A massive scarf wound around Cathy's neck and trailed down her coat. "What a miserable day. I thought we were through with this."

Rosie'd forgotten their lunch date. She breathed deeply, bringing herself back to the present. She gave Cathy a forced smile.

"What's the matter? Too busy to go?" Cathy asked.

"No. I'd like to get out for a bit." Rosie moved to the closet and pulled out her coat. She slipped into the coat, shucked off her shoes, pulling on high-heeled boots. "That last call was from this jerk I met years ago. I can't seem to shake him." She tried to laugh. "My fatal charm."

"Maybe you should tell Mr. McCallister."

Rosie answered quickly. "No, I wouldn't bother Daniel with it. I'm sure he's harmless. Just a geek. Don't worry about it. Feel like some really good Chinese? I'll spring for a cab."

"Sure, but I can't be late. Mr. McCallister's in a real mood today. I've never seen him so miserable."

As they rode the elevator down, Rosie pumped Cathy for information as to why Daniel was unhappy.

"Oh, he'd never say anything to me," Cathy told her, "but he placed several calls to his house this morning and no one answered."

FOUR

Daniel attempted to read the papers spread on his desk but could not focus on any one thing for more than a minute. He tried to think back to the months before his marriage to Sylvia, when the abortion must have taken place. How could he not have known she was dealing with such a major decision? Why didn't she confide in him? He'd thought they were as open to one another as possible; certainly he'd harbored no secrets. Since she'd acted unilaterally in a decision that affected their entire lives, what else might she have undertaken? Sickening doubts nibbled at the corners of his mind. He banged the desk with a fist and strode to the window. He breathed deeply and exhaled, shoving his hands into his pockets, frustrated that there was nothing concrete to lash out at.

The face of the young boy in his dream floated before his eyes. God, will I see it in my sleep again tonight? Sylvia's decision was irreversible, rendering him emasculated. The situation reminded him of his early years when decisions were made for him by his parents and his only recourse was to swallow the consequences.

He and Sylvia had met as freshmen in college and through her he'd developed a social life. Up to that time he could not recall having a steady friend other than Matt Pugnetti whom he met in high school. Matt had swarthy skin and a blue-collar father, automatically making him an unfit companion for the son of the city's mayor.

"Matt's not a friend you're going to need later on," his father would remind Daniel. "You need to cultivate people who will be a help in the future."

"So his family doesn't have much money—"

"It's not about money, Daniel. It's about influence. No matter how you prepare yourself, success is all about timing and connections. Without those two things you can be easily defeated."

Now, standing in his office, Daniel recalled one of his comebacks. Burning with the innocent zeal of youth he'd spit at his father, "I don't intend to run for mayor, you know! I don't need to be constantly worried about being defeated." They'd been out on the front lawn on a summer evening, their voices rising. Daniel had shouted those last words so the neighbors could hear. He had tasted a rush of impudent joy, though aware it would not go unpunished. His father made him choose between playing basketball and having Matt as a friend. It was not an easy choice, but basketball won because only on the court did life make any sense.

How ironic that he was now a part of the same white man's game that he had reviled as a young man. Matt Pugnetti, with all his charm and quick intelligence, would never even be given a chance to prove himself among the king-makers who had brought Daniel along.

Daniel sat back down at his desk and forced his mind to the matters at hand, but could not shake his mood.

The intercom buzzed. "Yes?" he said.

"It's Rosie. Have you got a few minutes to look over the speaking schedule for next week? We've got a conflict."

"Sure, come in."

Rosie, always efficient, took the visitor's chair, crossed her legs, and started right in. "The city planners want to see you on Thursday at eleven about the number of parking spaces for the shopping center. That will probably run into your noon speech at the Chamber. I called the Chamber. They have someone they can get on short notice, but if you cancel it will mean you won't be able to address them for another month."

"Let me call Jerry at the city planner's office. Maybe I can move that meeting up an hour."

"Want me to do it?" Rosie asked.

"Thanks, but he's a buddy. I think I'll have a better chance."

Rosie looked at him closely. "You look like you didn't get much sleep."

"None." Daniel rubbed at one itchy eye.

"Problems with politics, or with the business?"

"Neither."

"Oh," Rosie said, and Daniel noticed that she seemed to relax back into the chair just a trace. Her eyebrows raised slightly and she smiled at him. Daniel could not ignore her direct gaze.

"I've got some aspirin in my desk. Would that help?"

"Thanks," he said, "but I doubt it."

"Not getting the flu?"

Her head tilted and her eyes went soft. Surely she wasn't flirting with him.

"I'm sure it's not that, but I think I'm going to call it a day." Rosie didn't move, but kept studying him. He stood and began putting on his suit jacket.

Rosie slowly rose from the chair, smoothing her slim skirt over her hips. It was a velvety fawn wool skirt that clung to her legs. "See you tomorrow, then," she said.

Sylvia sat across the dinner table from Daniel, the only sounds those of silverware clicking against china. She picked at her meal, waiting for an opening. Over the last two weeks Daniel's demeanor had given her little opportunity for conversation. To Sylvia's surprise, he broke the silence.

"How's the symphony doing?"

It was safe, neutral ground. Not the track Sylvia was heading for, but it was a start. She was a volunteer fund-raiser for the Junior Symphony and they'd had a couple of lean years.

"Not great. We're thinking of an old-fashioned dance early in the summer," she recited without emotion.

Daniel resumed eating. "A dance?"

"A family affair. Everyone brings their kids. In a pavilion, outdoors, with a fiddle band."

"Will that raise much money?" Finished with his meal, Daniel laid his fork and knife precisely across his plate and picked up his coffee.

"Well, we can get the band and the accommodations donated, and probably some refreshments. Besides the entrance fee, we're thinking of a marathon dance, where you buy chances on which couple can stay on the floor for the longest stretch. There'd be one for the kids, too, which I think would be a lot of fun." Thinking about these enthusiastic youngsters, her voice took on some animation. "Of course we'd have to monitor them so they didn't try too hard. Some of them are pretty competitive." Sylvia thought especially of a young male violinist and a female cello player. Both had high aspirations and intensity to match.

Daniel drained his coffee. "Well, the company can make a substantial contribution next month." He half smiled and began to push away from the table. "If you'll excuse—"

"Danny," Sylvia interrupted, reaching across to touch his arm. "We have got to talk about the abortion."

He stood. "What is there to say?" He began to turn away.

Sylvia tensed. Frustrated and frightened, she spit the words at him. "For God's sake say *something*. Be decent enough to let me know what I'm dealing with."

He glared down at her. His mouth opened. He seemed to start in one direction, then shifted to another. "The act itself was bad enough. And all these years we've lived with this lie between us. But to jeopardize our chances at having more children?" He shook his head.

"Danny, that's nonsense. I had a perfectly safe procedure. I would never have done anything less, never taken chances with our future."

"Our future? Yours, you mean. If you recall I wasn't even consulted."

Sylvia stood and moved toward him. "Danny, won't you try to understand? You were so involved in your classes, you took everything so seriously sometimes I thought you'd split apart. I couldn't imagine you having to deal with it."

His voice was caustic. "Oh, so it was all for my benefit?"

She dropped her eyes. "No, of course not. I didn't feel ready to be a mother." Then she looked at him again. "And we weren't married."

He flung his arms out in frustration and railed at her. "You know I'd have married you!"

She spoke slowly. "Yes I know you would have. And my fear was that it would be with the same anger you just showed me."

He shook his head slowly. "You'll never understand," he muttered, turning away.

"I don't know if I've actually asked your forgiveness. I want to do that now. I know I should have consulted you."

"You didn't consult me, because you knew I'd have wanted that child."

Her voice rose again. "How could I have known? We'd never discussed it. At that time I had no idea how important having a family is to you."

Daniel took a deep breath. He spoke in disjointed phrases. "You knew I was an only child. A lonely child. And you know my folks, how unbending and inflexible they are. Well, they didn't become that way in old age, they've always been that way. They didn't let me have much of a childhood." The sadness in his tone struck Sylvia's heart.

Daniel continued, his eyes gazing into a void between them. "I was so lonely that as a kid I created an imaginary brother for myself. Brian." He turned away from her and moved to the window. "And, as I grew up, I promised myself one day I'd have a big, noisy family."

Sylvia took a few steps toward him. "But we didn't talk about it."

As if he'd not heard her, he continued in a droning, flat voice. "And now the first, and maybe the only one, of those children is already dead."

Sylvia sat heavily in one of the chairs. She could muster no further defense, and Danny left the room.

FIVE

The skinny ten-year-old boy shifted his heavy social studies book to his other arm. Behind him, the other kids shouted goodbyes to one another as they peeled away from the school toward their homes. He had the farthest to walk and the distance qualified him for a bus ride. But he seldom rode the bus; you had to sit too close to people. The boys teased him about his short haircut and glasses, and a couple of the girls stuck up for him, making it worse.

He was glad no one else lived near him or knew which house was his. Their street was shabby. Two blocks down it was really nice, then you turned his corner and saw rusty cars, dying lawns, skinny dogs. Of course they didn't even have a real dog at their house. His dad didn't like animals. People are animals, Roger thought. He didn't allow himself to complete the connection.

He looked down the long block to his house and his breath caught. His father's car was in the driveway; he was home early. Roger's steps slowed. As his breathing became labored, the street lost its sharpness. The houses seemed to lose their structure and sway together, like in a cartoon. The sidewalk *was one long, smooth track moving him steadily to his front door.*

His fingers were on the doorknob when he heard a crash from inside. Something broke with a glassy sound. He stood still, holding his breath. Then his father's drunken voice shouted, "Bitch!" and his mother cried out, "Martin, no!"

As the boy moved through the front doorway he heard a sharp slap and a body falling to the floor. He crept carefully to the door of his parents' bedroom but the old floor squeaked, giving him away. Suddenly the door was yanked open and he was looking into his father's bloated face.

"Get out of here!" he screamed at the boy.

Roger stood his ground, trying to see around the bulk of the man, to his mother. His father raised a thick hand as if to strike him across the face. In defense, the boy jerked backwards and lost his balance. He flung his arms back to break the fall.

Coming out of the dream, Roger smacked the backs of his hands—one against the iron headboard and the other against the wobbly bedside table, knocking it over. He cursed at the stabbing pain and the knowledge that the nightmares were becoming more frequent. It must be because his plan played constantly in his mind, demanding to be put into action. He couldn't delay any longer.

It was still dark, the room cold. He forced himself back into a fitful sleep and woke with the first light of day, with a terrible headache. After downing his pills he pulled on a T-shirt and jeans, then a heavy jacket, and went out for a newspaper. Returning, he unfolded it on the table.

In the second section he found a small article which mentioned that Daniel McCallister would speak to the Cattlemen's Club, the Junior Achievers and several other groups over the next several days. That meant McCallister would not be leaving town. Perfect. From habit he cut out the piece and started to paste it into the scrapbook next to the picture of McCallister and Sylvia at the convention center. Then he stopped, scissors in hand.

"To hell with it," he said to Mangy, who peeked out from under the corner of his bedspread. "No more clippings. I'm going to make so much news that Daniel McCallister will have enough material for a scrapbook of his own."

At the stroke of nine o'clock he picked up the phone and dialed the car lot. Within seconds Al's voice boomed over the line. He was in his usual sunny frame of mind. "What do you want, Bollinger? I got things to do."

"With this weather, business is in the toilet. How about I take a few days off, get some skiing in."

"Hell, yes," Al said, "it'll save us on coffee."

That night Roger slept well and woke before his alarm. On first waking he always laid still for a moment, fixing the day in his mind. When it registered that this was the day, his heartbeat quickened. He sat up and took a deep breath to calm the urgency in his body.

From the bottom of his closet he pulled a shovel he had bought a week before. Then he went down to his storage unit in the basement and hauled out skis, poles and boots. It was still dark outside and his fingers ached from the cold as he strapped the skis onto the car roof.

Back in the apartment, he whistled as he packed for the trip. His eyes ranged over his suitcase, checking its contents. He took a sheet from his bed and crammed it in.

"Oh," he said to Mangy, "can't forget the diary. No, we mustn't forget that." Mangy ignored him. She was getting a head start on the several dishes of food and a giant bowl of water on the kitchen floor.

Roger took the diary from its place on top of the scrapbook. He carefully cut out the page where his mother had referred to him as her blonde angel, folded it, and put the single page in his breast pocket. With a kitchen towel he cleaned the diary's cracked surface and carefully tucked it into a corner of the suitcase.

He bent down to pet the cat's head, causing her to hunch down. "You be good. I'll be back in a few days."

He drove west, the sun a pale eyeball rising behind him. Wind whipped the thickly falling snow into distracting flurries, streaking it across the highway and smudging the edges of the road. Roger's mind kept leaping ahead a day, plotting, and several times during the agonizingly slow drive he was jerked back to the present by sliding on black ice that lurked below the swirling snow. He paid his fee to the park attendant, an attractive middle-aged woman who sat in a warm booth. Fifteen minutes later he was entering the town itself. Vacancy signs on every motel spoke of the terrible weather.

He chose a modest hotel where he'd stayed once before. A fire burned in the grate, adding some grace to the cramped space that served as a lobby. Roger was disappointed when an elderly woman checked him in.   Last time there'd been a petite brunette in charge.

"You're one of the brave souls," the older woman remarked. "Not too many skiing in this cold."

"Only time I can get off work," Roger explained.

"Well, we're glad to have you."

Roger knew the town well, but to make conversation and set himself in the woman's mind, inquired where he might get a late breakfast. She sent him a mile down the road to The Alpiner.

The mock Swiss chalet with stained wooden beams and checkered curtains was empty. He took a booth and immediately the lone waitress, thirtyish and puffy-eyed, appeared.

"Mornin'," she said, handing him a menu and pouring rich coffee into his cup.

"What's good?" he asked.

"Waffle with sausages is my favorite."

"Fine." Roger handed her the unopened menu. "And two eggs over easy."

She smiled automatically and moved back toward the kitchen.

The clang of cooking pans was sharp in the silence. Roger would have liked some company, even at a distant table. Loneliness was something he expected when at home but hoped to avoid whenever he left it. He feigned interest in the faded color photographs on the walls—the Alps, he assumed, though they looked very much like the Rockies which towered just outside. As he sat back, he saw a crude carving in the table's edge. Long ago a pen knife had cut into the soft pine. The initials D + S curled inside a wobbly heart. Lovers must have sat here, he thought, rubbing the age-softened edges of the grooves with his finger. What did that kind of romance feel like?

"Here you are." The waitress placed two plates in front of Roger then came back to refill his coffee.

He ate hungrily, pushing away sentiment. There were things he would never experience; he'd accepted that long ago. When the waitress cleared the table he asked her if there were any good movies playing. "I might need something to do this evening."

She chuckled. "Haven't seen a grown-up movie in three years. I only take the kids to Disney. But there's a newspaper in the back; I'll get it for you."

Roger circled a movie he'd already seen, and left a tip she would remember.

Back in his room, he pulled out the phone book and called for a rental car. The company delivered it and Roger parked it at the back of the motel. He draped the sheet he'd brought from home across the floor of the trunk, transferred several items from his own car, and loosened the bulb so that the light didn't come on when the trunk opened.

Looking down from the chair lift that glided quietly above the frozen slope, the world was black and white—all snow and rock—and Roger felt like the only living being within miles. The lift moved into the cloud that shrouded the mountain top. Roger wrapped his arms around himself against the denser cold. He deeply regretted that his budget didn't allow him to ski an area with a nice warm gondola lift.

There were no shadows on the hill. This kind of light made the ski slopes seem flat, but there were no flat areas here. He'd have to be careful. He slid from the chair and his skis carried him downward quickly.

He found he could make only five runs, even though he stopped after each one to defrost his face and drink some coffee.

At four o'clock he gave it up and took the bus back to town. He returned to The Alpiner for dinner, pleased to find the same waitress on duty.

"You've had a long day," he said.

"I'm off in a half hour. I'll miss the evening rush," she joked, her laugh echoing in the empty room. "Did you decide on a movie?"

Roger mentioned the one he'd already seen.

After dinner he went to the theater and bought his ticket. Back in the motel, he tore it in half, stuck the stub in his shirt pocket and flushed the other half down the toilet. When he transferred his mother's diary from the suitcase to the deep pocket of his jacket, his hands began to shake.

By six o'clock he was back on the highway in the rental car. It could have been midnight, it was so dark. Once clear of the mountains, and on the prairie again, the wind still drove the snow relentlessly across his headlights, mesmerizing him. He had to keep shaking his head to clear his mind. When he picked up tail lights from a large truck ahead, he locked onto them and simply followed.

With his mind somewhat disengaged, his thoughts turned to his mother. He always pictured her hovering close overhead. He could see her face clearly, still. Sometimes clear enough to spot bruises and tears. As a boy he'd asked her why they didn't run away.

"When you were two years old we did run away. We took the bus. But we didn't get far. He found us at a motel." Roger remembered her halting, dismissing details from the story. "It was bad, honey. Really bad. I didn't dare try it again. But he promised that he'd never hurt you, and he hasn't."

"Well, mom," Roger said, directing his voice upwards through the roof of the car, "after you were gone he didn't keep his promise. After he didn't have you to bully he started on me." Then he was sorry he'd said it aloud, as if she might have learned the truth, for the first time, from him.

As he rounded a hill, the blowing snow eased and the lights of the far-flung city suddenly popped up below him. Only a few more miles. His heartbeat quickened and he felt that buoyancy which had always accompanied his visions of the plan in action. Maybe the results of this night's work would allow him to live a life not bound by hatred and jealousies. Might he actually defeat his demons and become a free man? His body seemed to swell at the thought. In his new euphoria he thought the city lights resembled fistfuls of jewels scattered on a white blanket, promising better times.

He dropped quickly down into the maze of roads, crisp with hard-packed snow, and deserted. It took him only a half hour more to reach the street where he had lived as a boy. He slowed the car. The neighborhood was even uglier than he remembered. One corner street light was broken. The house right next door was boarded up. Luckily, the other neighbors' drapes were drawn, their houses dim.

He cut his headlights and pulled into the driveway, sitting for a moment to see if he'd drawn any attention. No one stirred. A low light flickered from behind a threadbare curtain in the living room.

Roger's boots crunched on the hard-packed snow as he moved around to the back of the house. Once again he stopped, listening. He heard only the

61

steady drone of a sports announcer's voice calling a hockey game. He moved as quietly as possible up the few steps to the enclosed porch. His eyes searched in the darkness for a rusty coffee can and found it beneath a battered chair. Awkward in his heavy gloves, he struggled to take a key out of the can. The screen door hung open, cocked at an angle, the mesh ripped to strings. He turned the lock then put the key and the coffee can back. He opened the door and stepped into the kitchen.

He braced himself to be assaulted by the memory of his mother. But there was nothing of her in this sour smelling room. Used dishes, opened cans, stained towels and a stinking dishcloth littered the filthy countertop and stove. Only one thing remained the same—the old wooden crate in the corner, filled with empty whiskey bottles.

There were no lights on, the only illumination coming from the TV set in the living room. Roger moved to the doorway and looked in.

There the man sat, intent on the loud hockey game, obviously hard of hearing. A shiver of anxiety crept along Roger's spine as he stared at the back of the man's head. He would only be in his late fifties, but thin strands of hair looped up from a shiny scalp. Against the screen's light, his ears stood out and his neck was scrawny.

The kitchen stench attached itself to Roger's woolly coat and accompanied him into the other room. It mixed with the acrid smell of stale cigarette butts. Roger walked slowly around the seated figure, at a distance, curious to see what the man had become. When he was abreast of the chair's left side the man jumped, startled.

"What the hell?" he shouted. He slapped his hands on the arms of the chair and started to rise. Then his left leg collapsed under him and he had to grip the chair with both hands to keep his balance. He raised his face to Roger and yelled again. "Who the hell are you? Get out of my house!"

Roger met his eyes and smiled, enjoying the sight of what time had done. His father's face was deeply lined and sallow, the skin drooping in dark circles beneath startled eyes. From his shirt sleeves skinny wrists protruded, seeming too fragile to support those huge hands.

"Sit back down, old man," Roger ordered.

The man swung wildly at him with one arm. Roger grabbed it in mid-air. His voice rose a pitch. "I said, sit down." He shoved the man hard and he flopped back into his chair.

Roger lowered the sound on the TV to a whisper and drew up a footstool, sitting face-to-face.

"See anyone you recognize?"

Connecting with those sadistic eyes, Roger felt his blood rush. The man looked hard at Roger. As recognition set in he curled his lips in the thinnest of smiles. Crooked teeth shone in the glow from the TV.

"I knew you'd be back," he said. His tone became superior, though his voice cracked and wheezed. "Knew you'd be back to pick my bones. Well, look around. All this will be yours some day." A chuckle began to rise in the man's throat, choked off by a wracking cough.

Roger leaped to his feet and grabbed his father's shirt front. "Don't you dare laugh at me, you bastard! I didn't come to claim any of your filthy leftovers."

Even as he struggled for breath, the man's surprisingly strong hands gripped Roger's arms. "So what have you come home for?"

Roger released the shirt and broke free of his father's grip. "You call this a home?" He picked up the stuffed ashtray and hurled it across the room. "I haven't come home. I've come to even the score."

Roger put his hands on either arm of the chair and moved close to his father's face. "I had hoped for a more even fight, cripple, but then that never bothered you, did it?"

His father grinned sardonically. Tobacco breath hissed at him. "Once a whiner, always a whiner. Take your best shot, boy."

Roger straightened and stared down at this abomination of a parent. Martin Beauchamp's eyes didn't flinch; they taunted. Here sat the man he hated with all his being, a man who deserved to die. At hand was the focus of years of dreams and months of plans, yet a sinking feeling came over Roger that maybe he didn't have the heart to go through with it. Not wanting his father to see his indecision, Roger turned away.

Too late, he heard movement behind him. Roger spun around. "Did you forget this?" the man roared as he lunged up from his chair. Roger saw the baseball bat arcing toward him. He ducked, but not fast enough. It cracked against his skull. Hands to his forehead, he stepped backwards and the coffee table caught the back of his knees. He fell hard.

His father moved over him. Roger looked up. The bat was raised again, poised to strike. Roger kicked at the man's weak left leg. The knee made a sickening 'pop' as it collapsed. The bat fell to the floor, Martin Beauchamp on top of it, screaming in anguish.

Roger was on him like an animal. A great strength entered his body; there was no hesitation now. The eyes that looked up at him flickered with a fear that fueled him further.

He repeatedly banged the man's head against the floor. "You killed my mother. You killed her. Well you should have killed me, too, when you had the chance."

"No, no," Martin Beauchamp shouted, his arms wrapped around his head. "The car accident killed her."

Roger smashed fists into his father's face but he squirmed like an eel and the punches did little damage. Roger's voice rose with the effort. "She was already half dead when you put her in the car to take her to the hospital. I think you crashed the car on purpose!"

"But I loved her."

Roger, straddling the body, stopped all movement and stared, unbelieving, into his father's now-watery eyes. "You *loved* her?"

His father nodded. "You never understood. Neither of you ever understood . . ."

Disgusted, Roger shoved himself up off the prostrate form.

His father hoisted himself on one elbow and Roger waited, for what? An explanation? Could a love like that be explained?

Then Roger saw his father's other arm sweeping behind him, reaching for the bat again. He kicked at the man's temple, knocking him flat. The killing urge flooded back. With his arms flailing, Roger kicked and kicked at the man's body until he could no longer lift his legs. He didn't notice at what point the body became unresponsive, inert, lifeless.

He slumped into the chair, his whole torso sticky with sweat. His gloved hands felt like goo. He looked at the still form at his feet and felt nothing for it.

His head began to pound. Gently, Roger felt at the bump on his forehead and his glove came away with blood. He sat up quickly. He picked up the baseball bat from under the coffee table. He could see no blood on it. Still, he got a towel from the bathroom and rubbed it thoroughly. Roger buried the towel in a corner with some others and took the bat into the bedroom, rolling it under the bed.

His father's bedroom was strewn with soiled clothes and graying linens, the windows heavily draped. Roger turned on a small lamp and moved to the closet. Deep in one corner he located some female things. His heart skipped a beat as he recognized his mother's flowered dress, still in its plastic bag. That dress had been as precious to her as a debutante's exotic gown. Then he spotted her heavy winter coat. The years had bent the hanger so that the coat drooped at the shoulders, like a body without hope. Crouching, and reaching into the closet, he placed the diary in its pocket, being careful not to disturb the thick layer of dust that made a gray line across the collar and shoulders.

Roger turned off the bedroom light. He made himself wait a half hour to see whether he had alerted any neighbors, then half carried, half dragged the body out the back door and through the porch. He dropped it at the bottom of the steps. With his jackknife he slashed at the frame around the lock, leaving the door open. Getting the inert body moving again took all his remaining strength. He could barely lift it into the trunk of the car.

As he backed into the street he was glad the hard-packed base and the blowing snow would make any tracks difficult to identify, even though it would be highly unlikely they'd ever trace them to a car rented ninety miles away. But he had no idea what level of sophistication the police had reached in this kind of investigating.

Roger drove around the corner and into the cul-de-sac near the old Ajax Storage building. He cut the engine and sat a few minutes. Nothing moved, and only the wind could be heard.

As Roger pulled his father's lanky frame from the trunk, it seemed all angles. Arms and legs caught on every handhold, every edge, as if he lived. "God damn you," Roger hissed under his breath, giving one last heave that deposited the body on the frozen road. Still cursing, but feeling anxiety creeping upon him, Roger dragged it toward its resting place—the four-foot mound of snow deposited at the side of the road by the city's plow. He began digging.

The weak moon gave off a bare suggestion of light; the shadows it created only hinting of depth. Clouds scuttled across its narrow plane. In the still, frigid night the scraping of the shovel in the crusty hard-pack sounded like the breath of a thousand dragons, and Roger constantly looked around in fear that he'd be found out. But no creature, human or otherwise, broke the frozen, gray palette. Only he moved, his back bending, his arms swinging, breath heaving. He glanced now and then at the warehouse, seeing himself crouched in pain, feeling the panic once again. He began to groan aloud as he shoveled, tears streaking down his cheeks. He called, 'Momma, Momma,' in muffled sobs and, weeping like a boy, buried his past.

Roger sat in the car for several minutes looking back at the burial mound, his breath catching. Maybe he wasn't dead; maybe a long leg would kick out of the snow. Finally satisfied, Roger drove off.

On the highway he was beset by scenes from the fight—his father's head bouncing on the floor, his mother's coat hanging there, defeated. He gripped the wheel tighter. Smelling his own sweat, he turned down the heater and cracked the window. The cold blast felt good.

It wasn't fair. He didn't want to feel guilty about this. He wanted to revel in his success. Roger tried to see his mother's face smiling down at him. But she wouldn't smile. With a shock, he realized that she would not be pleased. She would not approve.

The car drifted to the shoulder. Roger jerked the wheel. When the car spun, he turned into the spin and corrected its course. He drove in a confused state, sick at heart, trying to recapture the joy he'd always felt in planning the murder. He had avenged his mother's death. Where was his reward?

When he came within a mile of the park gates, panic almost made him turn around. He didn't expect anyone would be manning the booth at this late hour, but what if he was wrong? However, as he slowly approached, he saw no lights, and was able to drive through uninhibited.

Roger woke repeatedly during the night and spent long sleepless periods unable to put away the night's events. When daylight seeped between the motel room's drapes, he was glad. Parting them a couple of inches he looked for sunshine, but the skies were slate grey.   He groped his way to the tiny motel bathroom and was shocked at the size of the ugly purplish bruise on his forehead.   The old man's favorite weapon, that bat.   Roger stood taller and studied himself in the mirror, shaking off his earlier sense of defeat.   He had accomplished his plan without a hitch; he should be happy with that.

Returning to sit on the edge of the bed, he turned on the television.   The weather report ran continually, in two lines of print, below the picture. Colder yet, today.   Skiing would be torture, but sitting around doing nothing would be worse. Maybe, after all this, he'd move back to Vancouver where snow seldom fell.   He'd just need to sell a few cars; build up a little nest egg.   The thought buoyed his spirits as he dressed for the day.

The bus deposited him and one other person at the lodge at the foot of the mountain.   He scanned the mountain face.   The few brave souls out there were clothed head to toe.   Faces were covered with ski masks that allowed holes for eyes and a slit for the mouth.   It seemed the mountain was being attacked by a small band of bank robbers.

Roger jammed his skis and poles into a snow bank.   As he trudged toward the warmth of the coffee shop a skier, who'd just completed a run, brushed past him and swept to an expert stop just short of the steps.   He kicked at the release mechanism and jumped out of his skis.   Roger saw crystals of ice around the mouth of the mask and the man's eyelashes were frosted.

"What a day!" the man exclaimed as Roger came alongside.   They climbed the wooden stairs together. Inside, the man peeled off his gloves and struggled to pull the edge of his hood out from under his collar. Freeing himself from the confines of the mask, he ran his fingers through matted hair.

"You going up?" he asked Roger.

"I guess," Roger said. "Paid my money ahead of time."

"Yeah, you'd think you'd get a refund when the temperature drops this low," he said.

They stood at the counter waiting for the one kitchen employee to spot them. Roger's companion was about fifty, very fit, and beginning to thaw. The man chuckled. "Makes me want to move back to the coast. You ever ski Whistler?"

Roger nodded, yes. Whistler Mountain was close to Vancouver. He'd worked there for two winters as a busboy in the coffee shop, skiing on borrowed equipment. "In fact, I'm thinking of moving back."

"Really? Well good luck. And try to think of us poor souls back here once in a while."

They ordered their coffees, the indoor air humid and stifling. Roger pulled off his cap.

"Jeez, that's quite a bump you've got there," the stranger said, looking at Roger's forehead.

Roger blinked. "Oh, yeah," he said, stalling, automatically covering it with his hand. "I hit a tree limb yesterday. It's not as bad as it looks."

The man paid for his coffee and moved away. "Well, take it easy."

Off balance from having someone notice his wound, Roger downed his coffee fast and headed for the chair lift. The long ride up was sheer hell. The muscles of his arms and shoulders had been screaming all morning and now they tensed as the cold ate at him.

At the top of the lift, to his left, there was a hump, like the back of an old woman, that fell suddenly away into a near-vertical drop. He was familiar with it, and had skied it often, but he was not loose enough today. He began the sharp decline, picking up speed with every foot of distance. Suddenly he caught a ski edge. He tumbled, completely out of control. His body flipped around and the tip of one ski dug into the deep snow. His boot did not release and his knee was wrenched painfully as he twisted to an abrupt stop.

He barely had time to assess his situation before the safety patrol arrived. The first young man was followed almost immediately by two others with a sled slung between them.

"Don't try to move," he was instructed.

Two of them worked on the bindings. "Man, you need some new equipment," one of them said. "This should have released."

Roger's pain centered on his right knee, but he could feel muscles seizing up in his thigh. They freed the boot and the pain eased some. They strapped him quickly into the sled. It was a fast, bumpy ride down.

A small infirmary had been built under the steps of the lodge. The ski patrol captain did a cursory exam of the range of Roger's leg movements. Then he asked Roger to walk. The knee threatened to give out if he put his full weight on it, but he could limp around.

"I don't think anything's broken," the captain said. "But you'd better get it checked out at the hospital anyway. The bus will drop you there." They helped him load his equipment and wished him luck.

Roger was alone in the bus. He banged his left fist on the seat beside him in frustration, knowing he needed to stay for at least a few more days. They were going to be miserable, long days.

SIX

At nine o'clock in the evening, with most of the city's population cozied down in their homes, a half-dozen windows on the top floor of McCallister Plaza glowed yellow. Bent over his desk, Daniel concentrated on a thick engineer's report, absently rubbing the back of his neck. Headaches and body aches had become the norm since the beginning of the misery about the abortion. Sleep eluded him, making even daylight hours long and arduous.

He had turned almost all of the engineering firm's work over to his general superintendent, but this sticky problem would not be solved without his family connections and personal intervention. The city planning commission objected to the traffic problems the new shopping center would create. They wanted him to put a road along the back of the property which would lead some of the congestion onto a secondary highway. That would be expensive. Daniel wondered what favor he might ask in return. Maybe a second traffic light with a left turn lane off of the main road, leading into the center. Or, perhaps, a campaign contribution from some of his father's town hall cronies.

That thought, seeming to come from thin air, made him sit up straighter in his chair. Receiving favors, and granting their necessary paybacks, had always been his main complaint about those in public office. Yet, so quickly, he had slipped into the politician's mindset.

Not pleased with himself, he stood up and walked to the window. The ache that had started in his neck was piercing all the way down to the middle of his back. He slowly rotated his head. A sharp crack echoed in his skull and the pressure eased a bit.

He heard Rosie clear her throat. She had chosen tonight to do some overtime. He walked to her doorway and glanced in. Her tidy frame, with that bushel of red hair falling to one side, was perfectly reflected in the dark glass window. Hunched over several phone books and other references, she seemed totally unaware of his gaze.

The thought of what lay ahead—the competition, the challenge—quickened his pulse. Maybe he could use that adrenaline to defeat some of the negativity that had lately consumed him.

Rosie was well aware of Daniel's presence in the doorway, but she did not look up. In the quiet, her pencil scratched roughly against the paper, then snapped. "Damn," she muttered, reaching for another.

Daniel spoke teasingly. "You should see yourself. So intent that you're breaking lead."

She pretended to drag her attention from her task to look up at him. His tie was loosened, the first two buttons on his shirt undone. He looked vulnerable. She experienced the same jolt of physical attraction she had felt on their first meeting, when she had answered his advertisement for a personal assistant.

Having just received her public relations degree, she felt qualified. At the interview, sitting across the desk from Daniel, she regretted the severe business suit she had chosen in order to appear older.

He held her resume, such as it was, in his hand.

"Not much applicable experience," he offered.

"Not the kind I'd like to have," she said with an easy smile. "But I'm energetic, a quick study. Getting in on the bottom floor of a political movement sounds incredibly exciting."

He laid the single page on the desk and sat forward. When he looked straight at her, she found she couldn't look at those hazel eyes too intently without giving herself away.

"Well, to be honest, I have no idea how far this is going. Right now it looks promising, but I've got a couple of strong competitors. I have to warn you, the job could be over in six months if things don't go my way."

Rosie saw her advantage. An experienced person would not even want so shaky a position. "Well, then, you need someone like me. I'm willing to take that chance in order to get a start."

When he called her the next day to offer her the job she clamped her hand over her mouth to avoid shouting "hallelujah" into the phone.

Rosie leaned up on her elbows, well aware of what that movement did for her figure beneath the pink angora sweater, and smiled innocently. Their eyes held for a moment. He seemed to flinch; did she see a hint of desire? He looked away.

"Hungry?" she asked. He didn't answer immediately and the word hung in the air like an offering. Would he accept it? "I'd love a really good steak," she added.

Daniel brought his eyes back to her. "Sure. Let me see if Billy is still down the hall—I've got him making cold calls. He can join us."

Rosie smiled. Safety in numbers. Maybe he was nervous.

At the supper club, Daniel helped Rosie off with her coat. A fabulous scent rose from the warmth of her body. This was the first time they'd done anything social together and, even with Billy along, Daniel sensed the danger of breaking their strictly business pattern. The late-night supper crowd was well-heeled and well lubricated. The maitre d' acknowledged Daniel and took them directly to a choice banquette. The room was comfortably noisy.

"Nice place," Billy announced, looking around eagerly.

"First time here?" Daniel asked.

"Heck, yeah. I'm a college student, remember? The closest I ever got to a place like this was when I was temporarily engaged to a girl whose folks had lots of money. They threw us an engagement party."

"Temporarily engaged?" Rosie asked. "What happened?"

"Her girlfriend, Maureen, was invited to the party," Billy said, blushing right through his freckles, clear up to his hairline. "I couldn't see straight after we met. Crummy thing to do to a fiancee, right?" He looked sheepishly across at Daniel.

Daniel shrugged. "Affairs of the heart were not my best subject in college, either. And I don't know if you ever really conquer the material." Though he was only making meaningless conversation, he had a fleeting thought of Sylvia, and a sadness spread through him.

"Hey," Rosie taunted, "what do you mean by 'conquer the material'?"

Daniel forced a chuckle, trying to change his mood. "Oh, I don't mean conquer women," he said. "I mean the complexities of a relationship."

She met his gaze steadily. "I should hope so," she teased, leaning toward him.

With a shock, Daniel felt Rosie's hand on his thigh. The long overhang of the linen tablecloth hid the movement from everyone in the room. Her hand shifted toward the inner side of his leg. He took in a sharp breath as a surge of desire ran through his body. Guilt was the next thing he felt; then rationalizations tumbled into his brain as welcome as drops of dew on cactus.

The conversation had lapsed, and he felt Billy's eyes on the both of them. He leaned toward the young man, racking his brain for something intelligent to say, when their waiter appeared at the table. Rosie slowly withdrew her hand, leaving its burning imprint on his leg. As she placed her napkin in her lap, Rosie's arm brushed his. He felt seared. She smiled up at him, just touching her bottom lip with her tongue.

Daniel cut his steak, chewed and swallowed, and made conversation mechanically, his mind running to improper fantasies. He ordered another bottle of wine. And then a third. He knew he was setting himself up, and alcohol was a great guilt killer.

Daniel asked Billy how the telephone canvassing was going. "I know it can get pretty discouraging," he offered.

Billy had drunk a little too much. He spoke loudly, with a youth's enthusiasm. "Not at all. I love it. You get the real pulse of the people."

"And are we affecting their heart rates?" Daniel asked, smiling.

Billy answered as soberly as possible. "Absolutely. You get a Progressive Conservative on the line—he'll always listen. That party is so disorganized the average guy is disenchanted, worried even."

Daniel glanced at Rosie, who smiled back. Obviously Billy thought he was telling them news. He continued, "Of course, Gerrard's people are a tough sell. But those who might defect certainly lean in our direction. They'd never go PC. I'm definitely on the right team!" Billy looked at Daniel with admiration. He lifted his glass in a salute.

"Me, too," Rosie added. She clinked her glass against Billy's, then Daniel's. "We're going all the way."

At Daniel's request, the doorman hailed a cab for Rosie. Daniel opened the back door. He took her hand to help her lower herself into the seat and felt her press a tightly folded piece of paper into his palm.

"Dinner was great. See you in the morning," she said. From the rear window she waved back at the two men.

Daniel stuffed his hands into his coat pockets. He turned to Billy. "Thanks, Billy. Your hard work's really appreciated."

"Well, I just think you're what a lot of us young people have been looking for, Mr. McCallister."

"Daniel."

"Daniel . . . thanks. And thanks for dinner." Billy hesitated, then motioned with his arm. "Well, my car's around the corner."

"Oh, I'm the other way," Daniel said. "When will you be in the office next?"

"Saturday morning."

"Great. See you then." Daniel hitched up his collar against the cold and turned toward the parking lot. Once inside the car he flicked on the dome light and unfolded Rosie's note. Anticipating the message, his breathing speeded up. Her address was printed neatly at the top of the paper, then, in cursive, *I'll be waiting. Have been waiting.*

Daniel drove around the city for fifteen minutes, changing his mind every few blocks. Then he headed to Rosie's. He sat in his car a half block from the entrance to her apartment building. The lobby was brightly lit. He could see a man having trouble finding his keys, digging furiously in several pockets. Finally he found them and disappeared beyond the security door.

Daniel moved quickly, running down the sidewalk, misgivings dogging his heels. Once inside the lobby, he punched Rosie's buzzer. Within a few seconds the speaker clicked on and he spoke into it. The lock released. He opened the door and stepped out of the glaring light into the relative privacy of the hallway. He took the stairwell up the two flights. As he raised his hand to knock, her door opened.

Her hair was pulled up in a knot, with damp tendrils trailing on her neck. The sash of a creamy satin robe cinched her waist. Behind her the room was softly lit.

Without a word she touched his shoulder, ushering him inside. The door clicked shut behind him. Her eyes held his as she opened his overcoat. She pushed back his jacket and slowly pulled off his tie. Unbuttoning the shirt, she put a silky, warm hand on his chest.

Daniel sucked in his breath. Rosie loosened the sash on her robe. It fell slightly open. Daniel's eyes followed a thin line of flesh from her throat, down past the mounds of her breasts.

She wrapped her arms around his neck, holding her body back from touching him.

"What kept you?" she whispered.

He pulled her to him, his mouth crushing hers with fierce demands.

Rosie slept lightly, with a smile on her lips, and woke clear-headed with the first hint of dawn. The sun was rising on her best day yet. She'd dreamed of mornings just like this: a city apartment, her career finally in motion, an influential lover in her bed. The fact that the man was someone she could really fall for, was a bonus, not a requirement.

Daniel snorted loudly and woke himself up. He jerked up on his elbows and looked around, seemingly disoriented. When he met her eyes, Rosie thought she saw a flash of something awful. Regret maybe, or, God forbid, an apology. He looked at his watch.

"Shit!" he exclaimed. He swung his legs out and reached for his shirt.

"Oh, Gosh," Rosie muttered, stretching. "I'm sorry it got so late. I was asleep, too."

"My fault." Daniel pulled on his pants.

She watched until he was dressed. Then she got up and held his coat for him, the soft camelhair caressing her breasts. He hunched into the armholes then turned and kissed her forehead. He left quickly, without a word.

Rosie stood still for a moment, disappointed by his rushing away. When she turned back to the bed she saw herself in the full-length mirror. She straightened her shoulders, then stretched her arms up over her head and swung her hair. Well, it was a start. In fact, it was a damn good start.

SEVEN

Daniel and Sylvia's home, an imposing two-story brick structure with glossy white trim on shutters and eaves, was one of a dozen in an exclusive subdivision on the banks of the river. They valued the relative privacy provided by its location—well back from the street on a full acre lot. A long driveway curved to the front of the house, creating a considerable stroll from the street if one was on foot. Under its crust of snow the lawn now lay dormant. The first thaw would show bleak, yellowed grasses and muddy flower beds until, feeling reasonably safe about further freezing, Sylvia planted hundreds of dollars worth of annuals.

The master bedroom, upstairs, overlooked the back yard which was much shorter than the front, maybe a hundred feet down to the river. A four-foot high rock wall defined the back of the property and protected it against spring floods.

Moonlight etched lacy shadows of barren tree limbs on virgin snow, but the beauty was lost to Sylvia. She hoisted her shoulders to shift the weight of her white beaded gown. Staring at the flat expanse of snow that hid the river, she felt as displaced as the fish who'd been frozen out of their homes. Danny had not come home last night. She'd heard him creeping into the guest bedroom at dawn. He'd left a couple of hours later for the office, and returned home just in time to get ready for the evening. When she asked herself who he might have been with, only one possibility presented itself. Rosie. Beautiful, ambitious Rosie.

Sylvia moved to the mirrored closet and saw an elegant woman with fear in her eyes. She straightened her necklace so the emerald pendant hung perfectly between her breasts and tried a smile. The Association of Engineers' Black & White Ball was an annual affair they had attended the two previous years. She'd found it a little stilted because most of the couples were considerably older than they, but the group's support was immensely important to Danny's future now. They had to go to the dinner, and they had to appear happy.

Daniel's frustrated voice came from the adjoining dressing area. "Damn, I hate these things."

She knew he was referring to his contact lenses. She would have to confront him soon, but not now. Tonight was too important, so she answered him lightly. "Vanity, thy name is Daniel."

She walked into the dressing area and stood behind him. He was leaning over, re-rinsing a lens. Hurt as she was by his behavior, she still wanted to run her hands over his bare shoulders. His eyes met hers in the mirror. There was no softness in them; he seemed to challenge her to mention his late night.

"Not that I have to defend myself," he said, "but it has nothing to do with vanity. It's those damn flashbulbs, as you well know. They reflect off glasses."

83

He bent back to his task. "Besides, if the word vanity hadn't been invented before you came along it would have been born of sheer necessity."

The sharp ugliness of the words shocked her. Was he now associating the abortion with some desire of hers to keep her figure? She moved back into the bedroom. Maybe he's decided the best defense is a good offense, she thought.

"Speaking of necessity, how is Rosie?" she asked.

Daniel, contacts in place, walked over to the bed and picked up the tuxedo pants. "Fine. She has amazing organizational skills for someone her age."

"You cut it pretty close this morning. I'd say her organizational skills failed."

She watched Daniel's face. He attempted innocence, went wide-eyed, with a wrinkle of shock between the brows. She waited for the words of rebuttal. Instead, he sat down and pulled on his shoes.

Oh, God, Sylvia thought, it's true. She swallowed hard. She fought back a rush of tears and stuck out her chin. She wanted to sound strong, but her voice came out all edgy. "Really, Danny, you can be so transparent. That will be a liability in politics."

"Apparently it's a liability in marriage. But I guess I'd as soon be transparent as be able to hide something from my spouse for fifteen years, without so much as one little slip-up." He glared across the bed at her.

She met his stare. "Don't keep pounding me with that if you refuse to hear my side of things. And don't change the subject. Was last night a first?"

He jumped to his feet, exasperation in his voice. "Oh, for Christ sake, what do you think?"

"I don't know what to think. I never thought in a million years we'd be having this conversation."

"Well, neither did I." He walked to the mirror and ran a brush over his hair, then left the room.

She shut her eyes and took a deep breath. The weight of the dress was suddenly too much. She sat on the edge of the bed, crossing her legs. A white satin pump came into view. All the trappings of success. For what? She kicked off the shoe. Even though she'd marveled at Danny's intensity with his studies in college and knew he would succeed at whatever he chose to do, Sylvia never expected that his then introverted personality would fit him for public office. Her own father was responsible for Danny's recent nomination. Tom Halliburton, an influential behind-the-scenes politician, had seen in Danny something she had not—a need to prove himself to his father.

Danny called to her from downstairs, "The car's here." Sylvia rose from the bed, slipped into her shoe, and her role.

They settled into the wide, plush seats of the town car. As soon as they pulled away, Danny turned to stare out his window. Sylvia pulled her satin evening coat closer, watching his handsome profile. He'd been at the office as late as seven last night, when he called to say he would work through dinner. No doubt Rosie Jones had been there, too. Why had he done it? To punish her? Or, maybe there had been something going on between Danny and Rosie before this. No, she decided, surely she would have known.

But then, when she was wrestling with the decision that had brought this wall between them,

Danny had been unaware of her turmoil. How could two people, so in love, not read each other better?

They'd not lived together long before she discovered she was pregnant. After the first days of panic she tried to look at it sensibly. In her mind she played out the scenario of having a child. She tried to anticipate his reaction. First, the necessary marriage—would she ever know for sure if he wanted her without that incentive? For all their intimacy, Danny had never actually talked of marriage. Then, the added pressures of a family. With school and his part-time job, how could he fit fatherhood into an already cramped schedule? How much harder could he drive himself? For that matter, how would she manage? In order to finish school, it would mean looking to their families for a lot of help, something they had always prided themselves on not doing.

She knew a couple of girls who'd had abortions. They assured her it was simple, and Danny wouldn't even have to know. She wondered constantly what her mother might have advised, had she been alive. In desperation she turned to her father and it was awful telling him. She saw the quickest hint of disappointment in his eyes before he offered financial and emotional support for whatever decision she made. They talked at length in delicately guarded terms, but the message she received was that abortion was probably the simplest way out. She had no religious scruples about it, and no maternal instincts yet. For purely practical reasons she'd gone ahead.

A mild depression settled on her for six months. She didn't have nightmares or longings, or crying bouts, which she expected, but she knew she had gone against her nature, every woman's nature. She felt diminished.

She lost her spontaneity in sex and Danny noticed right away. "What's the matter, honey," he'd whisper, touching her in ways that normally made her come alive in seconds. She claimed fatigue, or an upset stomach, as often as she dared.

"You need a break," he offered.

So that summer they both worked two jobs so they could afford a vacation, and they flew to Acapulco. The first night Sylvia stood out on the hotel's tiny balcony and looked down on the frothy stretch of beach. She wore a flimsy silk skirt that shifted in the breeze, between and around her bare legs. Music and soft laughter drifted up from the open-air bar.

Coming from behind, Danny wrapped his arms around her and pulled her close. She felt his body respond. She turned in his arms, their bodies brushing together. She put a hand on either side of his desperately serious face.

"You are so beautiful," he said. "Will you please marry me?"

"We're here," Danny said, bringing Sylvia out of her reverie. The car pulled up in front of the Palliser, a grand old hotel on the Canadian Pacific Railway line. Sylvia immediately put a hand on his arm, slowing his exit from the car. "Do you remember when you proposed, in Acapulco?"

Danny frowned at her, whispering, "This is not the time or the place."

The driver had opened her door so she stepped into the crisp evening air. Danny came around the back of the car and took her arm. A few couples

Marlene Baird

were gathered at the hotel's wide entry doors, a good distance away. "Your proposal was only a couple of months too late," she said to him behind her smile as they approached the group. "It was that close, Danny, just a couple of months."

She felt a jolt run through his arm but he reached for the outstretched hand of a colleague and shook it vigorously. "Bill, good to see you again. And Marion," he added turning his full smile on a diminutive woman in her sixties.

Decades earlier the Palliser had been one of the most elegant buildings in the city, and much of its original charm had survived the refurbishing. The immense ballroom glittered with silver and crystal. Everyone was in black or white, of course, so the only colors in the room were the pale green walls, the gilt-edged woodwork, and the lucky brunettes. Sylvia felt overburdened and washed out, but she put on a dazzling smile and laid her hand on Danny's arm.

EIGHT

On winter mornings Gene Hawthorne had the unenviable distinction of being one of the first men at work in the entire city, starting his day before dawn. The pay was pretty good for a man with a tenth-grade education, and in the summer he went into the construction trade which let him sleep until six. His home was modest, with two bathrooms that never quite got comfortably warm, but his garage was double-insulated. With all the snow this year, if his truck didn't start every morning, a good portion of the population would be stranded.

He was up at three o'clock, and soon on the road in black and white stillness. At three-thirty he unlocked a quonset hut door and, with the help of a battery jump from his own vehicle, coaxed the engine of a snowplow into life. He climbed onto the frigid seat, pushed the cab heater to its highest setting, and started out.

The beginning of his route was an old part of the city whose gentle-faced residential homes now housed offices of lawyers and accountants. There were already mounds of snow at the sides of the roads which he enlarged, trying as best he could not to block driveways. Several small strip malls required a lot of maneuvering; Gene enjoyed jockeying the monstrous vehicle in tight spaces.

By early afternoon his arms were tired from shifting gears and levers, but he was almost finished. Only a short stretch of road into a poorer neighborhood remained, then back to the hut. He moved quickly past beat-up houses, not taking as much care about driveways. Most of the places looked like a car would be a real luxury. A cul-de-sac, where the city bus turned around, marked the end of his route.

His blade scraped just above the road's surface, its edge skimming the bank at the curb, tumbling the new snow up over the old. Gene felt a slight jolt—a hesitancy in the push of the blade. It creaked in objection to some impediment, then moved on. He plowed the road regularly and Gene was surprised there would be anything on this deserted stretch to cause the bump, or whatever it was. Curious, he checked his rear-view mirror.

He jammed on the brakes so quickly the engine died. Not believing his eyes, he leaped from the cab and ran back to take a better look.

Detective Jerry Sullivan had seen many unusual and gory scenes in his twenty-four years with the police force, but this was something new. The gory part was that the top of the man's torso was still buried in the snow bank, but a long left leg, in ripped and dirty brown trousers, sprawled out on the street, twisted like a pretzel. The blade of the snowplow had almost torn it from its socket, then the two-ton vehicle had run over it. The unusual part was that there was no blood against the blazing white snow.

"Well, he didn't feel anything," his partner, Michael Duke, said. "Frozen solid." Duke was twenty years Jerry Sullivan's junior and looked even younger. Sullivan almost hated Duke for his muscle tone, and definitely hated him for the lock of rich brown hair that fell over his forehead. Sullivan's favorite dream, including sex, was that he had a head of hair so full he could part it down the middle and it would wave down over each ear. He often woke up with a smile on his face until he ran his hand up over his bald dome.

"Hit and run?" Duke offered.

Sullivan shrugged, looking around, his gaze taking in the decrepit warehouse building. "Can't imagine much traffic on this cul-de-sac. Can't imagine anyone out for a stroll around here either. I'm going to talk to the snowplow driver again."

Gene, sick to his stomach—he could still feel the drag of the blade as it caught the man's leg—sat in his warm cab, watching the officers in the side mirror. As the heavier of the two detectives approached, Gene rolled down his window. The detective reached up and shook his hand, introducing himself.

"This your regular route?" Sullivan asked.

Gene nodded. "This winter, yeah. Cleared here two days ago."

"If the body'd been here then would you have known?"

"Yeah. I always take the same track. It would have been more exposed than it was today."

"Ever see much traffic in here?"

"None, except for the bus turn-around." Gene swallowed hard, beating down his queasiness. "Can I get going now? I'm 'way behind schedule."

The entire crime scene force had now arrived, photos had been taken, and the detectives waited while two meticulous forensics officers dug the man out. The second leg came, then an arm.

"Shit, he doesn't even have a jacket on," Sullivan said, pulling his own coat collar up higher around his ears.

"Derelict?" Duke said.

Sullivan shook his head. "I doubt it. There's lots of homeless shelters where a guy can get a coat in this weather." Sullivan's ample gut, with years of practice and a ninety percent accuracy rate, was telling him this victim didn't walk to his icy tomb. He rode.

One of the forensics officers waved Sullivan over. He pointed at the snow bank near the man's shoulder. "Shovel marks," he said. "Not ours."

Sullivan patted his belly, glad to be reassured that his instincts were not deteriorating as quickly as his body.

NINE

Roger pulled into the car lot, splashing mud. Winter's back seemed to have been broken. He saw Richard showing a young couple a cherry red '90 Camaro, a new addition since last week. Roger would have liked it himself. Wonder what Al needs on that one, he thought.

His knee still made him wince occasionally but it was improving. The hours in the motel room after the skiing accident, or sitting in coffee shops, had seemed interminable, but now that he was back, with other things to concentrate on, he allowed himself to feel hopeful about the future. And he'd not had a headache or a nightmare in five days.

Inside, Bud, a recent addition to the sales team since Richard had gone to work for a new car dealer, sat with Henry staring at the coffee machine, willing it to brew faster. "Some things never change," Roger chided as he came through the door.

Bud spun around. "Hey, no crutches?"

Roger tossed his coat on the rack. He rubbed at the bruise on his forehead. It was still ugly from the blow of the baseball bat. "Hell no. Just twisted my knee a bit. And I hit a tree limb. No biggy. What've you guys been up to?"

Marlene Baird

"Not much," Henry offered. "It's been real slow. You don't want to look sideways at the boss." He made a slicing motion across his throat.

Henry nudged Bud and pointed to a man parking in front of the lot. "You're up," he said. Bud grabbed his coat and ran.

The coffee maker gave out its last gurgle and Roger poured two cups. He handed one to Henry. "I haven't even looked at the news much. What's happening?"

Henry blew on his coffee and took a sip. "Oh, let's see. Two murders. A domestic—what's new? Cabin fever and booze. And one guy frozen to death in a snow bank. They found him when the snow plow ran over the poor bugger's leg."

Roger shuddered. "Christ!" he said. "When?"

"Tuesday. I guess he was there a couple a days. The first report was that he was some poor homeless sucker, fell into the snow bank and froze. But you know the news guys, they're always wrong the first time around. Turns out the police are really anxious to ID him—they're asking the public's help. Must be on to some dirty work." Henry's eyes twinkled, his eyebrows shooting up and down.

Roger made a point of sipping slowly at his coffee while his heartbeat speeded up. Moving to the window with his back to Henry, he rubbed his mustache and asked, "So they don't have a clue who this guy in the snow bank is?"

Henry reached for the newspaper that was strewn over the small table. He shuffled a few pages. "Here it is." He began to read bits and pieces to Roger. "Just under six feet, fifty to sixty years old, skinny, bad left leg—arthritis."

94

"And no one's reported him missing?" Roger asked.

Henry shook his head. "Huh-uh. Really makes you wonder about some families, doesn't it?"

Roger forced a laugh. "Not me. Nothing surprises me any more."

That evening, back in the apartment Roger paced anxiously, chastising himself. He smacked himself on the forehead with the palm of his hand. Identification, stupid. You forgot the ID. He had several moments of panic wondering what else he might have forgotten. He made himself sit still at the kitchen table and think.

He weighed the possible consequences of his action a dozen ways and decided it was safe. Looking up a number in the phone book, he dialed. On the first ring he slammed the receiver down. How stupid! He copied the number on a slip of paper and ran down the street to the nearest phone booth and dialed again.

It was the end of a long day and Detective Sullivan's back ached. He knew it was probably from carrying around that extra twenty pounds up front. He rubbed at his belly as if he could massage it away. "Coroner said the guy in the snow bank had been beaten pretty badly," he said to Michael Duke.

Duke looked up from his paperwork and graced Sullivan with a full-fledged yawn.

"Jeez, thanks for all the interest," Sullivan chided.

"Sorry." Duke's hand came up to cover his mouth.

"You need some rest," his partner suggested. "Hasn't that baby settled down yet?"

Duke shook his head, his hair moving on his forehead. "Doctor says it's colic. Not much to be done. But tonight is Wendy's shift. Maybe I'll get lucky and get some sleep." He pushed his taut frame up from his desk. "Can we get out of here?"

Sullivan rose slowly and pulled on his coat. "Yeah, let's go."

They were about to clear the door when the phone rang.

"Sullivan."

"About that guy in the snow bank."

Sullivan grabbed at Duke's arm, motioning him not to leave.

"Yeah?"

"Sounds like a guy I used to know. Martin Beauchamp."

"Who is this?" Sullivan asked. He got a click for an answer.

Duke waited for an explanation.

"Anonymous caller," Sullivan explained. "Thinks he knows who the ice man is."

Duke's eyes lost their weariness.

"I hate anonymous calls," Sullivan muttered, "they always create more questions than they answer." He sat down at his desk and pulled out the phone book. He flipped to the appropriate page and read aloud. "Only one M. Beauchamp. Must be him. Let's go."

They drove slowly along Hudson Street, cursing at broken streetlights that made the house numbers difficult to see. Finally they spotted the house.

Their flashlights picked up no footprints or disturbances in the new snow. They knocked on the front door, then moved around back. The kitchen door had blown open. A snow drift, iced around the edges, leaned up against the stove as if for warmth.

Beauchamp's wallet, with an outdated driver's license, lay open on the kitchen counter.

"Don't move anything," Sullivan unnecessarily reminded Duke.

They flicked on lights as they moved through the house. The TV played to an empty chair. They noted the dashed ashtray and overturned coffee table.

"No one here," Duke said, after making a quick tour of the bedrooms.

"Let's tape it and put on a watch for the night."

The next morning a full crew went over the Beauchamp house. Forensics was finishing up when Sullivan and Duke started interviewing neighbors.

Duke found a talkative elderly lady a half block away. She eagerly invited him in, insisting he sit at the kitchen table. Duke refused a cup of coffee and tried to get to the point. "Mrs . . .?"

"Oh, I'm Mildred White. My husband passed away fifteen years ago."

"Mrs. White, we're investigating a possible murder." She put the coffee pot down without pouring herself a cup and sat across from him.

"Do you know Martin Beauchamp?" he asked.

She put one blue-veined hand over her heart. "Well, not really Mister Beauchamp. We never spoke. But I knew his wife, Maryanne, and their little boy, Roger." She peered at him with pale eyes, a frown creasing her forehead. "It's not Roger, is it? Who was killed, I mean."

"No."

She sighed in relief and sat back, her hands in her lap.

"It's Martin Beauchamp."

She just looked at him with no reaction. He continued, "Where are they now? The wife and the son?"

Her voice went melancholy. "Oh, poor Maryanne died a long time ago. It was a terrible car accident. I think little Roger was about eleven or twelve then. Her death was awful for him. Awful." Duke made a note on his pad and waited for more. "He was such a sweet boy. Maryanne often told me how smart he was."

She paused, remembering. "Then after his mother died he changed; became surly. Hardly even would wave to me. Then, a few years later, he disappeared."

"You never saw him again?" Duke asked.

The woman shook her head.

"Do you have any idea why he left?"

Her chin fell to her chest. Duke stared at the thinning white hair on the top of her head. She picked at fuzz balls on the sleeve of her sweater. He let the silence work for him. Finally she spoke, very quietly, her eyes asking Duke to understand.

"Sometimes the neighbors who lived closer would hear awful arguments—fights, really. I knew there was violence happening. Sometimes Maryanne looked pretty bad. You know, bruises." Her voice trailed off. "I knew I should have done something."

Duke came to her rescue, wanting her to continue. "There's probably nothing you could have done." He waited just a moment. "Do you think the boy was being abused, too?"

"I don't know, but after he ran away I never forgave myself for not finding out."

"How old was he then?"

"Fifteen, sixteen, I guess. High school."

"Didn't Mr. Beauchamp report him missing?"

"I don't know. No one ever came by making inquiries. And like I said, Mr. Beauchamp didn't speak to any of us. I always hoped Roger'd found some relatives to take him in."

"When did you see the father last?" Duke asked.

The woman blinked, trying to recollect. "Maybe a couple of weeks ago. He hasn't been going out to work for several years. He limps; maybe he gets some disability. I only see him go out for groceries now and then."

"Did he have any visitors?"

"Never."

"You haven't seen anyone near the house in the last few days?"

She shook her head, then touched Duke's forearm. "Are you going to find Roger now?"

"If we need him for more information."

"Will you tell him I said hello?"

"Sure," Duke assured her.

Sullivan sat back in his chair, frustrated, thinking out loud for Duke's benefit. "This is a beaut. No motive—certainly not robbery. No prints. The slashes in the door were obviously for show. He may have let the attacker in. Or, maybe the door wasn't even locked. Coroner says heart attack brought on by trauma. The body was bruised, especially around the head and torso. So why haul the body out and bury it?"

"To hide it?" Duke put in.

"Naw. Snow melts. Anyway, seems like the body could have been left in the house. No one would have found it for God knows how long. I think the killer wanted it to be found."

"Then why bury it at all?" Duke asked.

"To confuse the time of death? He was frozen solid."

Duke nodded. "Possible."

Sullivan switched gears. "I got next to nothing from the neighbors. This guy kept a real low profile. How about you?"

"An elderly widow, Mildred White, knew them."

"Them?"

"There is a son who left home at fifteen or sixteen. The wife was killed in a car accident when the kid was young. And there's a reason this guy might have wanted to keep a low profile, not mix with the neighbors much." Duke paused for effect. Sullivan waited impatiently.

"He was a wife beater. Might have abused the kid, too."

Sullivan grunted. "This woman have any idea where the kid is now?"

"None. Never saw him again."

Sullivan's tone was sarcastic. "Great. He won't be too hard to find. All these years on the run. Still, he might be our only clue. Might know about some old enemies."

"Maybe he is one," Duke added.

Sullivan nodded slowly. He rubbed the top of his head. "Could be. We need more to go on. You take a couple of guys and go back to the house. Get into every corner."

Duke returned to the precinct at six o'clock, a shoe box in hand. Sullivan looked up from his littered desk. "Anything?"

"Not much. There was a key in a coffee can on the back porch. Murderer could have found it, but it doesn't seem likely."

"Unless he knew it was there," Sullivan offered.

Duke nodded. He held out the shoe box. "Found these photos in the closet. There's a school photo of the kid we might be able to use."

"And?"

"This guy was a real bastard, Jerry. The wife kept a diary."

He reached into his jacket pocket and took out a small, worn book. He tossed it on Sullivan's desk. "We found it in the pocket of an old coat. She had hidden it, for good reason."

Sullivan looked up. "Prints?"

Duke shook his head. "Nothing useable."

Sullivan picked it up, riffling through the pages. "Erratic handwriting."

"Tough reading in more ways than one," Duke said. "You wouldn't want your kids to get a look at it."

Sullivan paged toward the end. Struggling with the handwriting, he read aloud. "I told Roger about the McCallisters. I'm too sick to help him now. I pray God will help him find them." He looked up to Duke for clarification.

Duke shrugged. "No other reference to that name, in the house or elsewhere in the diary."

"Sounds familiar," Sullivan muttered, then read a few entries to himself, his face growing more grim. He put the diary aside. "Jesus," he said, "I'd have killed him myself."

He reached for the school photo of the boy. "Have Jimmy add twenty years to this face and give us something to broadcast."

Duke started out, photo in hand. Sullivan stopped him with an afterthought. "You asked all the neighbors if they made that phone call?"

"No one admitted to it."

TEN

Rosie piled off the bus with two dozen other commuters and walked the half block to the office. The city's public transportation system was first-class and she was glad not to have the expense of a car. At just before seven o'clock, she was one of the first in the building. The security guard sat at his desk, his head nodding in what looked like a painful angle for his neck. All she could see was the top of his head.

She knocked lightly on his desk. "Hi, Andy. Tough night?"

He jerked upright.

"Gee, I'm glad it's you who caught me napping, Rosie," he apologized. "My sister's in town and I didn't get much sleep yesterday." He stretched long arms overhead then checked his watch.

"You're in early."

"Couldn't sleep," she said.

Andy twisted around and lifted a newspaper from the stack behind his desk, handing it to Rosie. As the elevator glided silently upward, Rosie's thoughts returned to where they'd been most of the night, with Daniel. That night spent at her place might never have happened; he'd been acting exactly the same to

103

her as he had before. She tried her best to match his coolness but underneath she was bothered. It was obvious he thought he had made a mistake, but she wondered if that was definitely the end of it, or if the timing had been bad. It disturbed her that he could carry on as if nothing had happened, but she wasn't ready to confront him. She had no intention of letting anything interfere with this job.

Disembarking on the top floor, she passed through Cathy's area and moved down the hall past the engineers' cubicles and the draftsmen's tables toward the small kitchen, flicking on lights as she went. After starting the coffee, she settled back in her own office, glancing quickly over the first page of the newspaper. Nothing pertinent. But, when she opened the paper, she was shocked to see a drawing of Daniel's face on page three. The caption jumped out at her. Police Searching for Son of Slain Man. Her head jerked back as she tried to make some sense of it. Daniel's father, Gerald McCallister, dead? The next statement added to her confusion. The police were asking the public's help in finding the man in the drawing. The face was Daniel's, and he certainly wasn't in hiding. Rosie shook her head. It made no sense. Frowning, she reached for the phone.

Daniel entered the kitchen, dressed for the day, the newspaper under his arm. The breakfast table was set immaculately—one cool green place mat, a pink grapefruit half and a small bowl of flowers beside the coffee carafe. He had hoped Sylvia would join him. He poured himself some coffee and energetically stirred a spoonful of sugar into his cup, slopping a few drops into the saucer. Guilt nagged at him, but he pushed it out of his mind. As a lonely child he had learned that it was painful to explore below the surface; better to keep busy, move on to the next challenge.

The telephone on the sideboard rang.

It was Rosie, almost breathless. "Have you got the morning paper?"

"Yes."

"Turn to page three."

Puzzled, he spread the paper. His mouth fell open as he stared at his likeness. He scanned the article quickly.

"What the hell?" he blurted into her ear. "It makes me look like a criminal or something. Get Barry Levy."

"He's in Jamaica, remember?"

"Oh, yeah, that's right. Let him be. I'll take care of this myself." He jammed the phone down, ripped out the offending page of the paper, and bolted for the door.

On hearing a door slam loudly, Chief William Greenburg glanced up from the work on his desk. He saw Daniel McCallister's dark scowl from across the squad room. Daniel strode into his office waving a page of the newspaper.

"I know why you're here, Daniel," he said before McCallister could erupt. "I've just got off the phone with your dad." He pointed to the page in Daniel's hand. "I didn't even see that drawing before it went to the press."

"Damn it, Bill, this couldn't have been a better match if I'd posed." Daniel held the page up next to his face.

Greenburg did a second take. "Jesus!" he said. "It's uncanny."

"Who the hell did this sketch?" Daniel demanded, smacking the back of his free hand on the paper.

Greenburg stood to add strength to his words. "A very talented young officer did it. For God's sake, Daniel, it's only a drawing."

"And it's only my career . . . with my face plastered all over the place as though I were involved in a murder." Daniel tossed the page on Greenburg's desk.

"Wait a minute," Greenburg cautioned him, anger at the edge of his voice. "No one said anything about charging anyone with murder in that article. We just need this guy for information. Anyway, no one would think it was really you."

"No? What does John Doe know about my private life?" Daniel paced away from Greenburg, then returned to the attack. "There's enough here to plant plenty of doubts. And God knows what Gerrard's people will make of it."

"Daniel," Greenburg interrupted, finally out of patience. "You can't be serious. No one is going to make anything of it. They'd be laughed out of town."

Daniel took a deep breath and sat down heavily. "I hope you're right." He paused. "It's just that this is such an important time for me."

Greenburg moved around the desk. He patted Daniel on the shoulder. "We'll pull it after today. It's a real long shot anyway; this guy could be in Timbuktu. But I've got to warn you, it'll be on all the evening television broadcasts tonight."

Roger smiled as the sketch of Daniel's face filled the screen. The blonde anchor announced that the police were asking the public's help in finding the man in the drawing.

"It won't be long now," he murmured, reaching out to stroke Mangy behind the ears. She twisted away from his touch.

ELEVEN

Detective Michael Duke hung up the phone with a sigh. He pushed his hair back and let his hand sit on top of his head. Sullivan looked over at him. "Bad news?"

"That was Wendy, from the hospital. It's not colic anymore, it's pneumonia. They're keeping Amy overnight for observation."

"That doesn't sound good. You get on down there," Sullivan demanded. "She needs your support."

Duke didn't hesitate. He pulled on his jacket and headed for the door. "Thanks."

His hand was on the doorknob when Sullivan stopped him. "Oh, just for your information, Greenburg's pulling that drawing of the Beauchamp kid."

"Why?"

"Seems it looks like that politician, you know—" Sullivan waved his fingers as if he could waft the name into his brain. Duke waited while Sullivan searched for the words. "You know . . . head of that new political party."

Duke flung the door open, his voice echoing his frustration. "So a drawing looks a little like some politician. Are we supposed to stop doing our jobs?"

"Not a little like. Exactly like. Let me find you a picture of the guy." Sullivan reached down to pull an old newspaper from under his desk. He began to leaf through it. "I'll look at it later," Duke said, moving through the door.

"Okay." Then Sullivan found the picture. He shouted after Duke. "Here it is. I'll leave it in on your desk. Guy's name is McCallister."

The next week the two detectives pulled an all-night stakeout. Well past midnight, Duke snored while Detective Sullivan contemplated his bad luck. When he opened the thermos, steam escaped and immediately the car's windshield clouded. He brushed at the moisture with his coat sleeve.

The coffee aroma woke Duke. He stretched as far the car would allow and yawned. "See anything?"

Sullivan poured himself some coffee. "Nah. Who'd go out on a night like this? I think we're here because the Chief is still pissed about me beating him bad in poker the other night. Hey, how's the baby doing?"

"Fine, thank God. It's been hell, but she finally got a clean bill of health yesterday."

"Glad to hear it. Give Wendy my best."

Duke reached for the thermos, hesitated, and stuck it between his legs without pouring any coffee. He spoke slowly. "On the Beauchamp case—"

Sullivan laughed. "What, you dreaming about it now?"

"That politician, McCallister, I saw him on TV last night. I can see why he was so upset about Jimmy's drawing. It was dead on."

Sullivan nodded.

Duke continued. "Remember the diary we found in the house?"

Sullivan turned toward Duke, issuing a small, impatient sigh.

"The wife's last entry mentioned the name McCallister. She said, 'I told Roger about McCallisters.'"

"I thought about that. Not an unusual name," Sullivan countered.

"But, with the drawing, it's quite a coincidence, don't you think?"

Sullivan sighed. "Look. McCallister is obviously not this runaway kid, Roger Beauchamp, so what's your point?"

Duke raised his eyebrows. "Let me dig a little?"

Sullivan spoke sharply. "Mike, that's all I need. The Chief's made it crystal clear that this guy is not to be bothered." He paused. "Look, all we've got is a flukey age-enhanced drawing and a name in a 20-year-old diary. There's nothing here, and I don't need the Chief on my ass. Let it alone."

Duke poured himself a cup of coffee without comment. Sullivan was a great guy to work with. He was smart, intuitive, easy to talk to. But his competence made it tough for any partner of his to shine. Duke wanted to do some independent work, something that was all his. He hadn't had a chance to really prove himself. Maybe this was it.

TWELVE

Daniel, phone to his ear, listened to some bad news from the site of the shopping center. He leaned well back in his chair. His superintendent, George Adams, always made things seem worse than they were; the best way to handle George was to let him vent.

As he swiveled toward the window, the brilliant snow-topped mountains seemed close enough to touch. He pictured these young, sharp peaks stretching from Alaska to New Mexico and wondered how far south you had to go before the snow disappeared.

There was a quiet knock on his door and Barry Levy stuck his head in. Daniel waved his lawyer to a seat across the desk, then spoke into the phone.

"No, George. No short cuts. Dig it up and start again." He paused to listen. "I know. We'll eat it. Better now than later. Call me tomorrow."

As Daniel hung up, Levy spoke. "You going to miss that engineer's hat you're wearing? It's time to get you into the limelight full time."

Daniel stood, rubbing his hands enthusiastically, smiling broadly. "Don't worry. I'm ready." He thought Levy looked especially crisp today, his newly

111

acquired tan at its best against the white shirt. But then, his small frame was always immaculately turned out. "Hey, aren't you back early?"

"Rosie faxed me that drawing. I got back as soon as I could."

Daniel shook his head in amazement. "Can you believe it? Such bad luck. But I told her not to bother you with it."

"You know Rosie," Levy said.

Daniel continued, "Well, I talked to Chief Greenburg right away. They pulled the picture immediately."

Levy's shoulders relaxed. "Great. Then we can move on to the next matter."

The lawyer sat back in his chair, crossing one leg over the other. Obviously he was waiting for Daniel's full attention. His tone went serious. "How are things with Sylvia?"

Daniel perched on the edge of his desk, sensing a conflict. "No real problems. Why?"

Levy ran the fingers of his right hand over the back of his left. Daniel recognized the delaying tactic. Levy connected with Daniel's eyes and spoke slowly. "Daniel, you've got to be squeaky clean."

Daniel nodded. What was this about?

"We were lucky with this police picture debacle— the Chief being a friend of the family. But it reminded me that Gerrard's people are running scared and they're digging like moles. Any of your missteps will be in the media before you even have a chance to address them."

Daniel slid off the edge of the desk and stood. "What are you getting at?"

"Gerrard's well aware of Sylvia's father's influence in the party. You make a much bigger target as a

112

calculating suitor than as an innocent college kid who accidentally married into his future." Levy paused. "In short, they'd love nothing more than to make your marriage look like one of convenience."

Daniel flared. "But that's preposterous! I had no political ambitions at all when we married. I loved her. That was it."

"And, now?"

"I still love her."

Levy seemed to relax. "Good. That's what I wanted to hear. Then let's make it a little more obvious. She needs to be seen with you, often. And you need to look more at ease with each other. Can you do it?"

"Of course," Daniel assured him, but he couldn't meet Levy's gaze. He sat down behind his desk.

Just as Levy picked up his briefcase to go, a unique knock sounded on the door.

"Come on in, Rosie," Daniel said.

She came through the door, smiling. "I need you two together for just a minute." Then, glancing at both men, she hesitated. "Is this a good time?"

"Sure," Daniel assured her. "What is it?"

Rosie opened the folder she was carrying and laid it out on the edge of Daniel's desk. Daniel stared, once again, at his own face in newsprint. "A reporter from the Herald has noted your similarity to the likeness and is making obtuse threats. Nothing specific, but I think he's looking to get himself a headline."

"I thought we told everyone we had no comment?" Daniel asked.

"Yes, but this guy's a comer. I'm afraid if we don't give him something he's going to write it his way, which will no doubt include lots of innuendo and little fact. I've drafted something, but wanted to get your ideas."

Rosie read her suggested response. Daniel nodded his approval, turning to Levy for confirmation.

"That sounds okay," Levy said. "Just emphasize that we never heard of the name Beauchamp, and assure this joker that this is an exclusive statement, and he'll never get another one if he changes one damn word."

Levy stood. "I've got to get going. I'll see you first thing in the morning." He fixed Daniel with a piercing look. "Remember what we were talking about."

After the door closed behind Levy, Rosie sat in his vacated chair, crossing her legs. "What's going on? That sounded like some kind of warning."

Daniel cleared his throat and spoke carefully. "He's concerned about Sylvia and me. He thinks Gerrard is going to try to make me into a fortune hunter if there are any hints of problems in our marriage." He gave a self-deprecating grunt. "Tarnish my good boy image."

"Does Barry know about us?"

Daniel tried to answer easily, while he inwardly shrank from her using the word *us*. It seemed to imply more of a relationship than he felt. "My experience with Barry is that he knows everything about everybody. Don't ask me how."

"Look, Daniel" she said, "I don't ever want to be in the way of your success. I won't do anything to hamper that."

Daniel saw that she was misunderstanding his reasons for avoiding more contact with her, but he saw an escape hatch and dived for it. "It's possible I'll be watched pretty closely."

"You know I'd rather you get elected than anything." She pushed herself out of the deep chair and walked around behind him. Daniel's skin tightened as she traced her finger across the back of his neck and whispered in his ear. "We'll have plenty of time. Afterwards."

The boldness of the act, in the office, made him realize her strength. She would be a formidable enemy and she deserved the truth, but self-preservation won out over chivalry. All he said was, "Is everything set for the dinner in Edmonton?"

She walked back around the desk. "I'll change your room reservation to a suite and have champagne and flowers waiting. Maybe some other snoopy reporter will get wind of it."

Sylvia slid into the limo at the airport in Edmonton for the first of a half dozen major fund-raisers planned for the next few months. The driver had recognized them immediately, welcoming them by name. Clearly Rosie's on top of everything, Sylvia thought, with grudging admiration.

Sylvia laid her head back on the leather bolster trying to ease a mild headache which had dogged her for hours. She was sleeping poorly, even though she felt more confident that there was nothing further between Daniel and Rosie. Daniel had been making half-hearted motions toward reconciliation, but the pain she felt about his betrayal was too fresh. And she needed a full discourse on the abortion issue, complete with his understanding, if not forgiveness, of her actions.

It was a long ride to the heart of the city and Daniel was making notes on his evening's speech. He put it aside for a moment and took her hand. "Thank you for coming along. I really appreciate it."

She pressed his fingers lightly, then took her hand away. "I'm glad to come," she said. They both knew she had little choice.

Finally the limo arrived at the underground parking area of a first-class hotel. Here, below street level, was a beautiful entrance, marble and brass, sheltered from the weather. Daniel turned to her. "This looks nice. Would you like to stay on an extra evening? A quiet dinner?"

"Let's see how things go," Sylvia said.

Sylvia unpacked slowly, waiting for the Tylenol to deal with her headache. Daniel was at the small table, his speech in hand. She heard him mumbling the words, saw him gesticulating, pausing where he thought it appropriate, waiting for applause where he expected it. He was definitely nervous. She felt a little guilty about her coolness in the car and called to him. "Barry told me they easily sold out the dinner. A hundred and twenty-five thousand dollars in one evening. Pretty impressive."

"Mmm," Daniel said. He picked up a pen and made a correction. He looked across the room at her. "How about I practice this speech on you. Like old times."

The familiarity grated on Sylvia; surely he didn't think it would be that easy. When she walked over to the table, he looked up hopefully, like a kid. For a moment their eyes held. She felt a stirring, and wished that things were different.

"Sure, I'll listen," she said, without a smile. She saw disappointment cloud his eyes, but he stood, backed away a few feet and began his presentation.

A sharp knock sounded on the door of the suite. Daniel walked the thirty feet and opened it. "Barry, what a surprise."

"We need to talk," the lawyer said in a low voice.

Sylvia caught his eye over Daniel's shoulder. "Hi, Barry. I didn't know you were coming up for this. Nice to see you."

Levy gave her a friendly smile. "Good to see you, too." He hesitated. "Look, Sylvia, I need to borrow Daniel for a few minutes."

"Sure. Want me to go away?"

"No. Of course not," Daniel said. He turned to Levy. "Did you get a room?"

"Yes."

"I'll just go down there," he said to Sylvia.

"I won't keep him long," Levy promised.

As soon as they were in his room Levy closed the door and turned to Daniel. He was scowling, his voice rough. "You ever try to find your natural parents?"

"What?" Daniel exclaimed.

"You heard me, you ever try to trace them?"

"No." Levy's look said he found that very strange. "What the devil is going on?"

Levy didn't answer immediately, rubbing one fist into the opposite hand. "Look, Daniel. When the party hired me I was told to dig. Find any hidden skeletons before the opposition had a chance to. How the hell could you not have mentioned to me that you were adopted?"

"I never think about it." Daniel's temper began to rise. "What possible difference could it make?" he snapped.

Levy turned his back.

Daniel continued. "To answer your question, no I never tried to trace them. They didn't want me, so I didn't want them. Simple. I've been happy with that."

"Sit down," Levy demanded.

Daniel sat on the edge of the sofa. Levy perched on the coffee table, leaning toward him. "Your natural mother was a Maryanne Scott. That was her maiden name."

Daniel couldn't believe his ears. What had this to do with anything? "Maryanne Scott?" The name felt strange on his tongue. "Maryanne Scott?" he said again.

"And she was married to Martin Beauchamp."

Before Daniel had a chance to put the two things together Levy continued, his tone still bitter. "The guy they found in the snow bank. Murdered."

Daniel shook his head. "Wait a minute." He frowned in concentration. His mind made a fuzzy connection with the drawing in the paper and its caption about the police looking for the son of the murdered man.

"Christ! That man was my natural father? No way. It can't be. Who dug all this up? This must be some of Gerrard's work."

Barry grunted. "I wish. But the opposition had nothing to do with it. Chief Greenburg called you. You weren't available so Rosie turned him over to me. One of his young, over-zealous detectives took it on himself to check you out, completely."

"But why?"

"The police found an old diary in the house of the murdered man. The wife, Maryanne, had mentioned the McCallister name in it. And, since you look exactly like the son who's gone missing, this rookie detective made the quantum leap of checking your birth records." Barry pushed himself up from the table, throwing his hands in the air. "I'd like to wring his g.d. neck!"

"A detective? Do the police now think I'm involved?"

"It's not quite that bad. Greenburg has a real tight grip on this now."

Daniel felt cold, knew he had gone pale. "How was my name mentioned in the diary?"

"Very vaguely. Only once. Something about how she told her other son about the McCallisters. Something like that."

Daniel's mind spun with the possibilities. What other son? Did he have a brother somewhere?

Levy went quiet, giving him time for it all to sink in.

Finally Daniel asked, "Where is Maryanne Scott?"

"I'm sorry, Daniel. She died years ago, in an automobile accident."

Daniel was surprised to feel his chest sink a bit. "And this Beauchamp. He's really my father?"

"He's named on the birth certificate."

Names on a birth certificate—a murdered man and a woman who died in a car accident. He'd found and lost both parents in a moment of time. Daniel blinked at the speed of it, his jaw dropping open.

A few minutes must have passed because Daniel felt Levy's hand on his shoulder. "Daniel?"

He straightened. "Do we know anything about him? My father?"

Levy hesitated. "He was poor. Lived alone after the son left." He sighed. "Not a nice character."

Daniel looked at him for clarification.

Levy took a deep breath, and seemed unable to meet Daniel's eyes. "Sorry, Daniel. He abused his wife, possibly the boy as well."

Daniel sank back into the plush sofa, staring at the opposite wall.

"I know this is rough, but we've got to keep moving ahead," Levy said. "The police want to talk to your folks about the adoption."

Daniel couldn't respond.

"Maybe they knew the Beauchamps. Maybe they can provide some kind of a lead to this son they're looking for."

Levy moved to stand directly in front of Daniel, forcing eye contact. "Look, this murder's got the police pissed. They've got so little to go on, they're grasping at straws. I'm sorry I ranted on like I did because I'm sure we've got no real worries. I was just upset that you hadn't told me about the adoption. I hate surprises."

Daniel ran his hands slowly through his hair and rose from the sofa. "I can see this getting real nasty," he said, finally. "A candidate with a murdered child abuser for a father."

Levy softened. "Look, I really don't think this will go outside the police department. You know the Chief's beholden to your dad. That'll be a big help."

Levy checked his watch. "Jesus, you've only got an hour until the dinner. You need to get going."

Daniel nodded and moved slowly to the door.

"You going to be okay?" Levy asked.

"Yeah." But Daniel's breath was coming in shallow bursts. "You have a seat for the dinner?"

"I do, but I'll skip it. I'm going right back to stay on top of this thing. Shall I call your folks? Prepare them?"

"Would you?" Daniel asked. "I'm not sure what I want to say to them right now."

An hour later Daniel entered the hotel's sparkling conference room to an enthusiastic welcome. He struggled to get a few bites of food down and get his mind back on track for the speech. But the generous diners did not get their money's worth. The applause was merely polite.

Sylvia tried to placate him when they got back to the room. "It was just one speech, after all," she offered. "But, please, Danny, tell me what's bothering you."

He started hesitantly, but soon the awfulness of the entire picture overcame him. Disconnected thoughts spilled into words as he confided his confusion about the past, disgust at his heritage from a monster of a father, fear of possible political consequences.

Only one positive thought emerged. "But I've got a brother, Sylvia, somewhere."

She put her arms around him. "Surely the police will find him."

THIRTEEN

Detective Sullivan squirmed. The living room was elegant, but stiff, like the chair he sat on. There were no magazines lying on the highly polished cherrywood table. No scent of coffee came from the kitchen. It made him wonder what this couple had been doing before he rang the doorbell.

Beverly McCallister, Daniel's mother, was older than Sullivan would have expected, attractive, with white hair pulled severely back in a roll. She was wringing her hands. Her husband's face was very familiar from his many years as mayor. He looked harried.

"Mrs. McCallister," Sullivan began, "I'm sorry if this will be upsetting."

She looked at her husband who gave her an encouraging pat on the hand. She spoke slowly. "No, detective. It's all right. I just want to explain. You see, we had everything arranged. We were to take the baby right from the hospital. The mother, Maryanne, had signed everything." Her voice began to waver. "But then, unexpectedly, she gave birth to twins."

Sullivan almost dropped his notepad. Out of the corner of his eye he saw Gerald McCallister squirm on his chair.

Beverly stopped to gather her words.

"One of the little babies was very ill. A respiratory problem." Her head sank to her chest and a harsh sob escaped her. "Oh, I'm so ashamed."

The ex-mayor put his arm around her shoulders.

"You see, we had planned on only one child and . . . and . . . we didn't want to take the baby who was so ill."

She began to sob loudly. Her husband looked at the floor. Mrs. McCallister took a tissue from her cardigan pocket and wiped her nose. She took a deep breath and tried again. "My conscience left me sleepless for weeks. When we finally contacted the hospital we learned the child was living with his natural mother. It seemed best, at that point, to leave things well enough alone."

Her red-rimmed eyes finally met Sullivan's, asking his understanding.

"How much did you tell your son?" Sullivan asked.

Gerald McCallister spoke. "Daniel has never asked about his natural parents. And he didn't know about the brother."

His wife turned tear-stained eyes to her husband. "Oh, Mac. He'll hate us. He always wanted a brother."

McCallister dropped his head and put one hand over his eyes.

Detective Sullivan waited for a minute. Then he addressed the husband. "So you had no contact whatever with Beauchamp? The father?"

"No, none."

Sullivan rose to leave. "I'm sorry about this. I'll contact you if we need to talk further, but it seems unlikely."

McCallister didn't rise, but extended his hand. "Thank you, Detective."

FOURTEEN

Roger sat across the desk from his boss. Al had called him in—an unusual situation that put Roger on edge. Spread between them were three contracts, the record of Roger's dismal performance at the car lot. Roger stared instead at the white cup rings and random scratches in the wood of the desk.

But Al seemed to be simply listing all his usual complaints, his costs of doing business—insurance, rent, licensing—so Roger relaxed a bit, let his mind wander. Then Al's voice took on a hard edge, getting Roger's attention. "So you see, you don't leave me any choice."

Suddenly Roger realized he was being canned. As it sank in, his thoughts raced. What the hell am I going to do? I've used up almost all of my unemployment. The car needs work. He began to sweat as his stomach churned. He forced himself to meet the other man's eyes.

"Jesus, Al, it's this rotten weather."

Al's eyes took on a squint that said he didn't want to hear any begging. His voice was firm. "I know it's been hard, but the other guys have put a few things together. In four months you've had three sales, two of which were repossessed."

Roger leaned forward, his fingers gripping the edge of the desk. "Hey, those repos weren't my fault. Those guys passed the credit checks."

Al stared at Roger's fingers until they were withdrawn from his desk, leaving wet prints.

"Yeah, yeah," Al agreed reluctantly. "Okay. But three sales. Pretty poor. We agreed, after four months, no more guarantee. I wouldn't be doing you any favors keeping you on. You'll starve to death on just commissions."

He paused and his voice softened. "Hell, Roger, it's not your game. You're too damn moody."

"I've got a lot on my mind," Roger said.

Al gave him a second to expand on that but there was only silence.

Roger lightened his tone, trying not to whine. "Look, give me a few more weeks. I know I can turn things around."

Al shook his head.

"There's nothing else out there right now."

Al stood up, ending the interview. Roger rose from his chair, anger beginning to boil in him. Al walked to the door, put his hand on the knob. Then he let go of the handle and pulled out his wallet. "I know it's rough right now. Here's a hundred—"

Roger smashed the money to the floor. "I don't need your damned charity," he hissed.

His mind in turmoil, Roger drove automatically through the hectic five-thirty traffic. He'd have to get another job real soon and he hated the prospect of hunting for one. His employment record was a laundry list of failures. His migraines had cost him many an opportunity—so many times he'd been unable to show up, or had come in late once too

126

often. His eyes began to skip along the business fronts for possibilities.

At a red light, a Pizza Brothers truck stopped beside him. Roger recognized the dents in the left rear fender. When he'd delivered for them, he'd backed into a cement abutment and they hadn't fixed it in over a year.

A block ahead the bucking bronco on the Rangeland Hotel sign was doing his act in red neon. Roger remembered a guy who worked as a bellhop there; maybe he could get a lead. When the light changed, he put on his turn signal and stuck the nose of the Mustang into the right lane.

In one of the city's oldest hotels, what was once a quaint western-style lobby now looked seedy. The dim yellow lamps no longer carried any decorator's mystique, but, instead seemed to say the establishment was saving on electricity. Roger approached the registration desk. A pretty, but tired, woman looked up. The glow from the computer screen gave her face a greenish cast. Her name tag said simply, Sherry.

Roger watched her practiced eye note that he had no luggage. "Yes?" she said. Her gaze slid over his face and fell away, disinterested.

"I'm looking for someone," Roger said. "Works as a bellhop."

"Steve's on his break." She pecked at the keyboard. The greenish cast changed to yellow.

"No, not Steve. His name is Abe. Abe Constanza."

"Oh, Abe." She turned away from the computer and gave him her full attention. She smiled, but Roger had the feeling the smile was not really for him. "How do you know Abe?" she asked.

"We worked together somewhere else. Do you know where he went?"

She splayed her home-manicured fingers on the counter and hunched her shoulders. She tilted her head and her hair fell to one side. "Maybe."

Roger was not fooled by her teasing. No doubt she was searching for information—probably had an unpleasant message for Abe—but she might be a good contact for a job.

"Look, what time do you get off?" he asked. "We could have a drink."

She looked at her Mickey Mouse watch. "In about an hour. Meet me in the bar?"

Roger ordered a whiskey with a water side while waiting for her. He seldom drank and the warm jolt of the liquor bolstered him. His worries diminished as he sat in companionable solitude.

Sherry arrived wearing a frilly pink blouse instead of the white cotton she'd had on earlier. She curled back into her chair, hitching her skirt. He bought her a drink and she closed her eyes briefly on the first sip. Between questions about Abe, she finished the whiskey with obvious satisfaction, then licked at the rim of the glass. She prodded Roger for details about where Abe had lived, whether he had family in the area. It was obvious she was desperate to contact him and was disappointed to learn that Roger really didn't know Abe all that well.

It wasn't long before Roger knew why Abe had disappeared from Sherry's life. She was a lush. She bought a couple of rounds, then he bought her one more drink before he was out of cash. Roger stopped drinking but that didn't even slow her down. The bartender knew her well, and apparently she was good for the tab, because the flow never ebbed. He knew there would be no connection through her to a job. He pushed back from the table and started to rise. "Nice to meet you Sherry, but I've got to get going."

She grabbed at his forearm and pulled him close. "Hey," she chided. "Don't be in such a hurry." She tried to sit up straighter. "Stay with me while I have just one more." Even though she didn't interest him, there was nothing to rush home to either. He sat back down.

"That's better," she smiled.

He felt the toe of her shoe running up the back of his calf. Even though she was a cheap broad, the motion stirred him. He knew better than to become involved with a woman; still, he relaxed back into his chair. His last encounter had been a waitress at the pancake house where he worked. He had moved into her apartment and things went smoothly for a couple of months. Then one night he wanted to go out without her, just for a beer. She demanded to know where he was going, and for how long. As they argued she clung to his arm. The screeching tone of her voice sent him into a frenzy and he smacked her hard with the back of his hand, sending her to the floor. She was a tiny woman, there'd been no need to get violent, but Roger, once again, had become his father. Following these episodes he stayed clear of females for long periods, and it had been many, many months this time.

By eight-thirty Sherry was bawling over some ancient lost love and any thoughts of sex, however fleeting, were eroded. "Look, Sherry, I really have to go. Can I give you a lift home?"

She looked in his general direction and forced her eyes to focus. "Oh, sorry. You must be one of those guys who hates tears."

She groped under her chair for her purse and came up with a tissue. She dabbed at the mascara and blew her nose. She smiled at him. "I'm fine now."

Roger stood. "Good. But I really need to be going. I'd be glad to drive you home."

Her face fell and aged five years. Her eyes turned dark as she smirked at him. "What's the matter? Don't you like girls?"

Roger's body stiffened. He felt an overwhelming urge to lean over and slap her stupid face. Instead, he gripped the edge of the table until his fingers hurt. Then, without a word he turned for the door.

He was half way there when he heard her yell out, "Don't forget to tell Abe to call me."

God, what a bitch, he thought, as he ran toward the car. He jumped in and slammed the door. He'd almost struck her. In public! Christ, he'd be in jail. He sat, numb at the thought, and, as the alcohol left him, a cold fear crept through his bones and he began to shake. Hating the sharp burn of tears behind his eyes, he turned the ignition with jerking fingers.

As he drove carefully toward home he realized he didn't have enough money on him to pick up dinner. There might be forty dollars in the bank, and the only thing he had coming was his severance check. He hoped Al would be decent enough to get it in the mail right away.

Suddenly desperate to see the want ads, and spotting a newspaper vending machine, he pulled the car to the curb. He rummaged in his pockets. Nothing usable. The drive home was a blur of anxiety. As soon as he entered the apartment he grabbed his jug of loose change and spread it on the table, searching for the quarters among a huge pile of copper.

After firing Roger, Al never gave him another thought until he pulled onto the lot the next morning. Then he shouted every curse he had ever learned. Most of the cars had two or three tires slashed.

Two young police officers arrived within five minutes. One continued to survey the damage as the other went inside with Al who was breathing hard from exasperation. Sweat beaded his upper lip. His voice rose in frustration. "It couldn't have been anyone else. He was really ticked. And he always was a moody pain in the ass."

"You might be right, but there's probably no proof out there," the officer said patiently, jerking his thumb in the direction of the lot. Al glared at him. The young man continued, unperturbed. "Any other guys you fired?"

"Not lately."

"Any of your customers unhappy with you?"

Al shrugged, "Who the hell knows?" he said, but his tone admitted it was a distinct possibility.

"An angry ex-wife?" the officer asked, trying to lighten the moment.

Al grunted in disgust. "Naw. Her style is to smash windshields."

The officer gave a sympathetic grin. "We're living in hazardous times." He folded up his pad and moved to the door. "We'll talk to this Roger

131

Bollinger, but if he lives alone as you say, there's not much chance we can prove whether or not he was out at some point during the night slicing tires. If you come up with anything concrete give me a call."

"Yeah, thanks," Al responded ungraciously.

As soon as the door closed Al picked up the phone book, checked a number and dialed.

The phone rang in the cramped office of a 1950's building. It made Dick Ellis jump, then flinch with pain. He was sixty-seven years old, with a drooping gray mustache which barely cleared the coffee as he sipped at his cup. He sat with his bad leg propped up on an overturned wastebasket. The ankle was swollen and wrapped loosely. The rest of him was tight and wrinkled. He spun his swivel chair a few degrees to reach for the phone.

"Ellis Investigating," he answered, stubbing out the last of his cigarette.

"Dick. Hi, it's Al."

Ellis's face lit up. "Al! Son of a bitch. Good to hear from you buddy. What's up?"

"You still in business?"

"Yeah. I guess. I come down a couple a hours a day. Marge says I get too cranky sitting at home. What about you?"

"Hell, yes. Wouldn't know what else to do. Listen, I got a little job for you. Interested?"

"Sure." Then Ellis' voice dropped. "But I got a bum leg right now. Gout. It's the pits. Painful as hell if I'm not all doped up."

"Sorry to hear that. Well, it's up to you. You probably wouldn't have to move around much."

"What's it about?"

"I fired a guy yesterday and last night he slashed all my damn tires."

"No shit. Everythin' on the lot?"

"Almost. Can't prove it, of course, but I know it was him. I'd love to catch the little prick on his next escapade. I'd like you to track him a little."

"Hell, I can probably do that without gettin' outta the car."

Al qualified his request. "I can't put a lot of money in it."

"Night work?" Ellis asked.

"Probably would be best."

"For nights, it would have to be weekends. Marge has been sick. On weekends her sister comes over to help out."

"Sorry about Marge, but when you do it makes no difference to me. Just whenever you can spare some time."

"Great. Gimme some details." Ellis had to make Al wait while he dug up a pad and pencil. Then he started writing, repeating back over the phone. "Yeah, Roger Bollinger, thirty-five, dark, mustache."

FIFTEEN

Newspapers covered the kitchen table, the Help Wanted ads on top. Over the years Roger had become too familiar with these. He quickly eliminated the dozens that promised easy money—they were either outright scams or semi-scams, known as telemarketing. That shortened the list considerably. He paced the apartment, coffee cup in hand, checking his watch every few minutes, but it was only seven, too early to start making the rounds. The cat meowed soulfully but Roger didn't want to spend what little money he had on cat food. He got a cracker out of the box and tossed it on the floor. She pounced on it.

When a heavy hand pounded on the door his heart stopped. He called out as firmly as possible, "Who is it?"

"Police."

Blood rushed to his forehead, setting it on fire. The room went gray and his knees almost buckled.

The fist knocked again, more insistently. "Roger Bollinger?"

Roger drew a noisy breath. He tried to sort out his thoughts, but panic made them gel into an incomprehensible blob.

"Open the door."

Roger put his hand on the knob and turned it.

The door pushed open against him, and he faced two uniformed officers.

"Are you Roger Bollinger?" the shorter man asked.

Roger's eyes darted from one face to the other. "Yes."

"We need to ask you a couple of questions," the man said. The other officer looked beyond him, studying the apartment.

Roger nodded, moving back into the room.

"Where were you last night?"

Roger almost dropped to the floor. "Last night?" he said, embarrassed that his voice sounded girlish in his relief. He pulled himself upright and said, "After work I went for a drink, then I came home. Why?"

"Where do you work?"

"Well, actually I got fired yesterday, but I was working at a car lot." Roger could hardly keep from smiling; they were only interested in last night.

"Did you return to the car lot after your firing?"

"No."

The other officer shifted a few pages of the newspapers on the table, looking underneath.

"Do you have a roommate or anyone who can vouch for your being here all night?"

"Only my cat," Roger said. "But I had a drink with a woman, Sherry, who works at the Rangeland. She'll verify that. What's going on?"

The officers exchanged glances. The one who'd been wandering around the apartment shrugged his shoulders.

135

"There was some trouble at the car lot last night. We're questioning the employees," the first officer said. "Thanks for your time."

Roger held his breath for a full minute after they left, then laughed. Someone had nailed Al. He would have given anything to know who and how.

At nine o'clock he left the apartment, still cheered by the thought of mischief, or worse, happening to Al. He stopped by the bank to change his coins and started on his list of jobs.

By three in the afternoon he was back home, tired and dejected. There were a lot of people after those few jobs. He'd had only one hopeful interview—a start-up company selling office supplies. He was to call back in two days after they'd had a chance to see a few more people.

Roger began clearing the newspapers off the table so he could have some dinner when a picture of McCallister caught his eye. He was out of town addressing a fund-raising dinner. Five hundred dollars a plate. That would pay Roger's monthly rent and his utilities, with a bit left over for food. McCallister's tuxedo fit like he was born in it. He certainly didn't look like a man with a murder charge hanging over him.

Roger had been counting on seeing more stories linking McCallister with the murder. Obviously the police had backed off. Well, maybe they needed some help.

Roger sat down over a lined writing pad. He wrote a few words, "To whom it may concern." He scratched them out and tried again. "I have information on the Beauchamp murder." Yeah, right to the point. Get their attention. He searched for the second line, but could not get it right. Disgusted, he ripped the page from his writing pad and balled it into a tight wad. He fired it at the cat, who deftly scooted under the couch. Roger got up, put on a jacket and left the apartment.

Across the street from McCallister Plaza he paced a half block in one direction, then back, then back again. It was the end of the work day and he was invisible amid the crush of people spilling onto the street from the many office buildings. He had no real purpose, only that he could focus his anger on the towering glass facade. He rubbed at his mustache in exasperation. The thought that Daniel was still enjoying his celebrity instead of sitting in jail made him sick. Clearly the stupid cops had not found the diary; he'd hidden it too well. That's what he'd do. Give them a clue. But how could he explain where to find it without implicating himself? Roger paced in frustration.

The weather was easing; the street and the sidewalks now dry in the traffic areas, with slushy snow along the edges. After a half hour the crowd began to thin and he felt a little exposed. He was about to leave when Rosie emerged from McCallister Plaza. She moved quickly, in sexy high-heeled boots, to a bus stop. On an impulse Roger dodged against the traffic to cross the street just as her bus pulled up. He barely had time to jump on before it pulled away.

All the seats were taken and the aisle was jammed. He pulled his collar up and turned away from Rosie, squeezing past her to be near the back door. After a few miles he saw her pull the cord for the next stop and move to the front. Roger was first in line to exit at the back. He jumped out onto the street and moved quickly away to his right. He checked over his shoulder. Rosie was going the other way. He slowed and turned just as she entered her apartment building.

A string of flashy new residential buildings had sprung out of the ashes of mom-and-pop stores obliterated by progress. He watched her enter the lobby and saw a brass panel of buttons, the kind used by visitors to signal people inside. There was an older woman in the lobby. She and Rosie seemed to exchange a few words as they picked their mail from their boxes. The confines of the small space gave the scene an intimacy, almost as if they were affectionate with one another. At some remark, Rosie tossed her head and seemed to laugh. Then she unlocked the security door and they both disappeared.

Roger watched the empty lobby, wishing Rosie would come back. He had never known the kind of camaraderie she and the older woman shared. He stood for a while, imagining how great it would be to have an easy friend like that.

The sun dropped from the sky, sucking all the warmth from the air. He turned slowly in a full circle. He searched for a bus, but wasn't sure where it would stop for his trip back to town. The couple of blocks he could see in either direction were barren of life. Everyone was tucked up inside their homes, behind those yellow lights, with family or friends. A street lamp above him flicked on. As he slowly walked toward downtown, his shadow, his lone companion, stretched ahead.

SIXTEEN

The prevailing westerly winds that strike Canada's western shoreline are warmed by the Pacific Ocean's Japanese Current, blessing the western coastline with moderate winters. And, normally, when the winds reach the Canadian Rockies they rise and cool, depositing rain on the western slopes, snow on the eastern slopes and out across the prairie. But occasionally, when clouds form a heavy blanket above the mountains, the warm air has no chance to rise and cool; it is compressed and funnelled through the mountain passes. It breaks free of the eastern ridges in the form of a whistling, warm wind that sweeps across the prairie, melting snow and softening ice within minutes. The temperature can rise thirty degrees in a half hour. School playgrounds are then strewn with coats and scarves as children free themselves of winter's trappings and race on legs sap-full of stored energy.

If it happens in early spring, golfers, who have spent winter hours putting into cups on the living room rug, are more than ready to test themselves on a course with barren patches and less than perfect greens. Golf course managers, whose season is far too short, take every opportunity to indulge them.

Marlene Baird

Sylvia was glad they'd finally reached the eighteenth green. She and her father had started the day in short sleeves, but a near-freezing rain had rumbled up when they were on the fifteenth fairway, and, even under her jacket, she was chilled through. Many other golfers had given it up, but her dad wanted to finish the round.

Huge drops slapped them in the face and flattened their hair. Sylvia putted out after her father. Tom Halliburton replaced the flag, and they dashed for their cart.

In the clubhouse lounge they chose a small table snugged up against the fireplace. Walnut and mahogany and crystal reflected the flames, while outside the sky darkened further. Sylvia studied her father's face in the fire's glow; it seemed more at peace than she'd seen it in some time.

In all the years since her mother's death, Tom Halliburton had never found a replacement for his beloved companion. For a long time Sylvia had feared he would kill the drunk driver responsible. Even as a youngster, she had been aware that her father was a powerful man, accustomed to wielding influence. But God had not seen fit to negotiate with Tom Halliburton as he pleaded at his wife's bedside, embittering him for many years. Still, he'd been beside Sylvia, strong and supportive, through every indecisive moment in her life. Well, she was in crisis mode with Daniel now, and needed her dad as much as she ever had.

Hail pinged against the windows. "God," he said. "Look at the pot holes that hail is making. I don't know how the groundsman keeps his sanity, trying to groom a golf course in this city. The weather is terrible in the winter and worse in the summer."

"It's nowhere near summer," Sylvia reminded him. "We're really pushing the envelope today."

"And being punished for our optimism," he returned. "But I really enjoyed the game."

Sylvia hated to spoil his day by bringing up her problems. She mentioned the Junior Symphony as a buffer.

"There's a great little guy from a needy family—a true prodigy. At ten he plays the violin like most adults. I know music should be his destiny, but it's a matter of keeping him on course. I'd love to hear what he could do if he had a really fine instrument."

As she spoke of their next concert, her father wrote out a check and pushed it across to her.

"I wasn't going to ask you for money."

"I haven't made a contribution for a while. Tell the powers that be that I wish it to go to help a specially-qualified youngster."

As Sylvia tucked the check into her purse, her father asked, "How is Danny holding up? I know it can be hard in the public eye. Lots of exposure, lots of people to please."

"He thrives on it," she said quickly. "I've no doubt he's going to lead this country one day."

"And you'll be fabulous at his right hand."

"He really believes in what he's doing, and people can sense that." She paused. "Oh, dear, doesn't that sound like I just read it off a teleprompter?" She took a deep breath and looked at him.

"What's the matter?" her father asked.

Sylvia leaned across the small table and spoke very softly. "Dad, couldn't you have prevented their digging so hard? Danny really lost it when he learned about . . ." She couldn't finish the sentence.

141

His forehead wrinkled. It took a moment before he understood what she was saying. "Has that surfaced?"

Sylvia nodded.

He reached for her hand. "Oh, honey, I'm so sorry. We naturally had to order background checks on all the candidates." He looked down at the table. "I didn't anticipate they'd be that thorough."

"It was fifteen years ago," Sylvia whispered. "How do they find this stuff?"

Sylvia saw pain in his eyes when he met her gaze. "It's my fault. I recommended the party hire Barry Levy because he's the best. Unfortunately we got more than our money's worth." The handsome face was tight with regret. "I'm really sorry, sweetheart. But surely Levy buried it again; few people will know about it."

"I don't even care about that. It's Danny. He's crazy with grief. And it's like we're being punished. We've been trying to have a baby for years."

"Give him some time. It must have been a terrible shock."

Sylvia studied the table top. She wanted to tell him about Rosie, just to have him console her, but there was no need to hurt him further.

"Honey, look at me. Maybe, at that time, your mother would have advised you differently—"

Sylvia stopped him. "No, Dad. Don't think that way. You've been wonderful. I'm sure you're right. Danny will come around."

Tongue-tied by their thoughts, they both looked out through the window. The hail had stopped as quickly as it started and a thick band of sun slanted across their table.

"Could this stupid speculation about the Beauchamp murder hurt Danny?" Sylvia asked.

"I've gone over this with Barry Levy. First of all, the public doesn't know his connection to the family. And even if it got out, I'm sure we could counter any attacks. After all, Beauchamp had no real influence on Danny, whose whole life has been exemplary."

Until now, Sylvia thought.

They finished their drinks and her father walked her out to her car. She waved goodbye with a smile, but as soon as she was alone the tears flowed down her cheeks.

As Sylvia approached the house she saw an unfamiliar car pulling away from the curb. She pulled into the long driveway then noticed that the other car had stopped, backed up, and parked again. She stepped out, and suddenly Danny was there, holding her door.

"Good game?" he asked.

A bald, middle-aged man was running up the drive, breathing hard. His raincoat fanned away from a wide belly.

"Who's that?" she asked.

Danny waited for the man to come closer. When he was within a few feet he introduced them.

"Darling, this is Detective Sullivan." He turned to Sullivan. "Detective, this is my wife, Sylvia."

"How do you do, Mrs. McCallister," Sullivan puffed, automatically showing his badge.

Danny spoke to Sylvia before the detective could say anything further. "He has a few questions regarding the Beauchamp murder."

Sylvia frowned. Her father had just told her this would not touch them.

143

Daniel took her arm and began to move toward the house. "Barry's inside," he said.

They sat in the living room, Danny hunching close to her on the sofa, both facing the detective. Barry Levy, leaning casually against the fireplace, gave her a reassuring smile.

Sullivan spoke directly to Sylvia. "As your husband indicated, we're still looking into the Beauchamp murder. The date of death was March 6 or 7. I need to know where you were those nights."

Sylvia flushed with confusion and concern. "Where I was?" She glanced at Barry, who nodded encouragingly.

Sullivan elaborated. "Actually, I need to know if your husband was with you."

Sylvia turned to Danny. Why would they care where Danny was that night? He gave her a half smile and a shrug. "That was weeks ago," she said at last.

Danny chuckled. "My reaction, exactly. So I checked our calendar. It turns out the Black & White Ball was on the eighth."

Sylvia sank back into the sofa, thinking. She nodded to herself. The night before the Ball was one she'd never forget. Daniel hadn't come home; but he certainly hadn't been out committing murder, unless one counted the death of a marriage. And the night before they'd spent a very quiet evening, he watching television and she in the living room. She looked directly at Detective Sullivan. "Yes, I remember. We were home on the sixth and the seventh and went to the Ball on the eighth."

"All evening? Together?" Sullivan asked, searching her eyes.

"Yes," she said levelly.

144

Sullivan stood. "Thank you both."

Barry Levy grabbed up his topcoat and walked out with Sullivan, turning to speak to Daniel and Sylvia. "I've got an appointment in a half hour. I'll talk to you in the morning."

When they were alone, Sylvia stood, head down, facing the cold fireplace, hugging herself. Daniel came up close behind her. He put his hands on her shoulders. She jumped at his touch and turned.

Danny's voice was entreating. "I hate putting you in this position."

Her flat gaze stopped him cold. "What's going on? How serious is this?"

He stepped back. "It's not at all serious," he said. "They have to dot all the i's and cross all the t's to put this thing away."

Sylvia turned back to the fireplace. "It would have to be that particular night."

She felt Danny come close as if to touch her again, then he dropped his hands. "Yes," he said quietly. "That was really bad luck. I'm sorry to have put you on the spot."

She twisted and looked over her shoulder, holding his eyes. "So there are times when withholding the truth is appropriate?"

"Sylvia, I'm so sorry."

She knew the apology covered a range of subjects but it seemed far too little. "Me too," she said as she left the room.

After leaving the McCallister's house, Sullivan met Duke at their favorite cafe. It was old enough that even Duke's long frame could drape comfortably in the bench seats of a booth. Sullivan slid his butt over grayed tufts of stuffing that poked up between the cracks in the vinyl.

Duke had ordered coffee and a plate of donuts. "Well?" he asked as soon as Sullivan sat down. "How'd it go?"

Sullivan shrugged. He picked up a coconut-topped donut. "No way to know. He's good. Smooth. Too much practice in the public eye. No way you'd trip him up. Said he was with her both evenings. But when the wife drove up he rushed right to her, almost as if trying to get to her before I could."

Duke couldn't hide his excitement. "Was he coaching her?" he said quickly.

"Well, there really wasn't time for that, but there was some hesitation, some silent communication between them."

"Enough to dig further?"

Sullivan shook his head. "No. The alibi is solid as it stands. At best I felt only a discomfort between them—could have been anything."

Duke didn't want to back down. "Still—"

Sullivan fixed him with a stare. "The Chief said to cover the bases and then put this away, and that's what we're doing."

Duke backed off. "Yeah, I guess I'm with you. I can't really see this guy doing the murder. But do you think he's being set up? Politically, maybe?"

Sullivan shook his head. "Would it make any sense for anyone to actually commit murder? Take that kind of a chance? Why not just expose the father for the jerk he was and try to make some press out of that." He ate half his donut in one bite, speaking through the crumbs. "Anything on the other son?"

"We thought we had a lead from years back, in Vancouver, but it petered out. He must have been terrified that the father would hunt him down. He disappeared real good."

Daniel lay in the dark, his body aching for sleep. The king-sized bed seemed a mile wide with Sylvia impossibly far away. When he asked if he could sleep in their room again she had hunched her shoulders as if to say, who cares? But he took it as better than a straight-out no. He wanted to hold her, but knew he'd be expecting far too much. The way she had come to his aid this afternoon, without hesitation, when their relationship was so strained, touched him. He had taken a hard look at himself and realized he was acting like a fool. The anger he felt about her abortion was real, but so was Sylvia's need for his forgiveness. He tried to understand the struggle she must have undergone before making such a decision. How could he not have seen her pain? And the night with Rosie—how much was punishing Sylvia for something she could never change, and how much was an ego trip brought on by his sudden success? He'd acted like a juvenile. Now Sylvia seemed to have run out of patience with him. Exactly what he deserved.

He craned his neck to see the bedside clock. Five a.m. He got up as quietly as he could, went downstairs to shower and shave. He dressed, picked up the suitcase and hanging bag he'd packed the night before, and left.

As he moved through the office reception area a bright flash caught his eye. Through the open door to his father's office he saw the early sun reflecting off the tops of the highrises casting everything in pink. He entered the office. His dad almost never came downtown any more, but they kept everything ready for him anyway. Glancing around at shelves of perfectly placed books, furniture geometrically aligned, Daniel shook his head. Everything in order just like his father's entire life. Except for the most important thing of all—it was inconceivable that in all these years his father had not told him about his brother.

He picked up a framed photo from the credenza. The same photo had sat on his mother's bedroom bureau for years. At the time it was taken, when Daniel was seventeen, he'd been embarrassed that his mother had called the newspaper and asked them to send several glossy prints of the picture. Now, as an adult, he could understand it perfectly. It was an unusually attractive picture of the three of them—his father, mother, and himself. They were at a tree-planting ceremony at a junior high school. In the brief moment captured in the camera's eye they were a beautiful, complete family. This was a case where the picture's fabled thousand words were mostly lies.

The day after that tree planting they had left on a family vacation. The long drive to the Grand Canyon was one unending geography lesson with no stops to actually get out of the car and do something. His parents were almost sixty then and they had long since lost what little sense of adventure they'd ever known. Daniel recalled all through his childhood wishing they were younger. His schoolmates went on mountain hikes and white-water rafting trips with their folks. He went to Quebec City to delve into the country's past, to Toronto and Washington, D.C. to study museums. No doubt a lot of that had been beneficial in the end, but he couldn't think back to any carefree times. He had never slept in a tent, wrestled with his father on the living room floor, or waded into deep water to fish.

When they finally got to the Grand Canyon he was forbidden to take the mule ride down the steep grade. His folks agreed it looked too dangerous. And there was no question of anyone going up in the sightseeing airplane since one had crashed two years before.

On the long ride home he fell into a black depression. For two days he sat sullen, looking at the backs of their heads, with years of anger fighting for expression. Sometimes, while he sat perfectly still and seemingly composed, he dug his nails into the palms of his hands so hard they left mean, red bruises. He ground his teeth until his jaws ached.

They had crossed the Canadian border and were only a hundred miles from home, when he could take no more. His father had asked him something. Daniel hadn't really heard the question and didn't care to, so he just grunted.

"For goodness sake, Daniel," his father lectured. "Perk up. Look around you. The world is a big place. There's no room for your petty moods."

Daniel exploded.

The words he shouted at them were so ugly his memory refused to save them. But he remembered clearly the incredible hurt in his parents' eyes as he raged. His father had to stop the car. At first his parents sat, dumbfounded, while he paced the side of the road with long steps, sweeping his arms dramatically, screaming at the top of his lungs. Years of swallowed retorts spewed from him.

Daniel shook his head slowly, remembering. It had been a pretty fair breakdown. He couldn't recall how long it had lasted, but he remembered fighting off their entreaties, shrugging away their touches, until finally he was reduced to a blubbering, sobbing heap by the side of the road. When he was physically spent they lifted him back into the car. His mother sat in the back with him while he cried aloud. When he began mumbling about Brian—his imaginary playmate for so many years—his mother cried, too.

Immediately after that he and his mother set out on a lengthy European trip, ostensibly to 'broaden' him. Of course the real reason was to make him sane again. He'd visited an exclusive hospital in London twice, for a month each time.

So many empty years. Daniel took a deep, shaky breath. Being dog-tired was making him weak. He put the photo back in its place and went into his office, closing the door.

Soon he heard Rosie arrive, then Cathy, then the normal buzz of people going up and down the corridors. He concentrated hard on several items Cathy had left for his signature.

His intercom buzzed.

"The car will be here in five minutes," Rosie reminded him. Her voice was flat.

Early on he'd promised Rosie she could be his travelling aide on this cross-country speaking tour; she would be, by far, the best point person he could have along. When Levy found out, that changed. "Take Billy," he'd said. "And have Sylvia join you somewhere, as soon as she can."

"Rosie will you come in for a minute? And see if you can find Billy. He should have been here by now."

A few minutes later Rosie entered his office.

"I can't reach Billy," she said. "Let's hope he makes it in time." Her tone said she didn't think much of Billy's chances.

"I'm sorry, Rosie. I know this was to be your trip, not his."

She shrugged.

Daniel continued, "Sylvia will join me in Toronto next week. Please call her, get her schedule, and make the arrangements." Rosie nodded, her face immobile.

Just then Billy burst into the office, coat on, suitcase in hand. "Sorry, boss. Had to drop my dog at the kennel. They were backed up."

Daniel pulled on his coat, picked up his suitcase and hanging bag and brushed past Billy. "Come on. That car should be here."

Billy, looking harried, closed the door behind them.

Rosie hugged herself in the sudden silence. She walked to the window ostensibly to watch them get into the car, but from this height she couldn't see directly below. She didn't hear Cathy enter the office until the door clicked softly. She turned toward her friend, blinking back tears.

"You're not crying?" Cathy said, incredulous. "I've never seen you cry."

Rosie brushed angrily at the tears. "Billy can't handle this and Daniel knows it. There are a million details to be worked out. The logistics of the speaking engagements alone are overwhelming. I've

Marlene Baird

been working on them for weeks and had to turn all my paperwork over to him." She sat down in Daniel's chair, gripping the arms.

"Why Billy?" Cathy asked. "What about school?"

Rosie threw her hands up in the air. "The baby's on spring break. Spring break, for God's sake." She bolted out of the chair. "God! First he kicks me out of his personal life, and now this. What next? A pink slip? I planned on being with him all through the campaign and the election. He needs me."

"Of course he does," Cathy agreed. "Surely this is just a one-time thing. How did he explain it?"

Rosie's voice dripped with sarcasm. "Oh, he needs me here to keep things in order, keep him in touch every day."

"I'm sure that's true."

"Like you can't take phone calls and open mail and relay messages." Rosie realized that sounded patronizing. "Sorry, I didn't mean that the way it sounded."

"No problem."

Rosie sighed. "I think I'm done here. It's only a matter of time." Then she looked up at Cathy, her voice hardening again. "But I'm not going without a hell of a fight."

SEVENTEEN

Daniel called twice every day during his trip; Rosie knew he was making an effort to include her in some of the decisions. While the difficulties that Daniel was suffering because he'd taken the wrong assistant gave her satisfaction, she was not placated. Time and again she upbraided herself about sleeping with him. The clarity of hindsight, true, but she'd certainly expected it to be more than a one-night stand. It definitely gave Daniel added incentive to keep his distance now. How much better it would have been simply to test the waters that night; to meet him at the door, in her robe perhaps, but then talk of business and watch his disappointment. She'd forgotten a key lesson for survival she'd learned on the ranch: give everything demanded, and not an ounce more.

Cathy came into her office, arms laden with mail which she put on Rosie's desk. "Can I bring you a coffee?"

"No thanks," Rosie answered, her voice short. When Cathy retreated, Rosie brandished her pearl-handled letter opener like a stiletto, ripping envelopes open as if she bore them a grudge. When the telephone rang she grabbed at it impatiently. "Rosie Jones."

"Hello, Rosie, it's Roger."

She cursed under her breath. "Roger, you creep, you said no more calls. I'm hanging up."

"Wait," he yelled. "I need to talk to you."

"Leave me alone." She smacked the receiver back on its cradle.

An envelope, addressed to Daniel, bore the words 'Private and Confidential.' She was accustomed to opening such missives—they were usually crudely disguised attempts to circumvent her sorting process. As she hurriedly slit the length of the envelope a photograph fell out, dropping to her lap. She picked it up and couldn't believe her eyes. It was a picture of Daniel in the lobby of her apartment building. It was a little fuzzy, but he could be identified. Quickly she searched the inside of the envelope for a non-existent note, then looked in vain for a return address. She turned the photo over. On the back was typed, "Wouldn't the press like to get ahold of this."

The incorrect usage of the word *ahold* registered as she sat back in her chair, staring at the photo, thinking hard. Then her eyes moved to her telephone. Roger, she thought. The jerk must be following me. I should have talked to him.

Roger cringed at the phone being slammed in his ear. "Damn!" he shouted, banging down the receiver. Surely the police had made the connection between McCallister and Beauchamp, but there was nothing in the press. He needed to talk to Rosie to find out what was happening with McCallister, and she wouldn't even talk to him.

Wildly, he kicked his way through the stacks of newspapers strewn around his living room. Soup bowls with food dried to their insides and glasses ringed with milk littered the coffee table. Cursing, he swiped at them, scattering them and their contents.

Rosie's tiny, well-lit kitchen sparkled, with shiny copper-bottomed pans hanging over the stove. But Rosie's mood didn't match the room. With no appetite, she stirred vegetables in the wok and sipped at a glass of wine. Daniel would be furious to learn of the photo. His anger would spill over to her, and whoever had taken it had control of both their lives. She felt very small and lonely in the island of light.

The lobby buzzer sounded. Surprised, she turned off the heat, moved through the living room and pressed the speaker. "Yes?"

A male voice whispered. "Rosie, it's Daniel. Let me in."

"Daniel?" Her heart speeded up. "Did you come back early?"

The voice was anxious. "Hurry. Someone will see me." She pushed the button, then waited impatiently at the door. As soon as she heard the knock she looked through the peephole. She smiled and opened the door.

Suddenly, the door was shoved hard and she almost fell backwards. "Daniel . . . what?" she began, gripping the knob and struggling to stay upright. The man moved behind her, grabbing her arm and twisting it up her back. He kicked the door shut. Rosie cried out and lunged toward her intercom. The man jerked her backwards, sending a blinding pain up her arm and into her shoulder.

"Shut up," he hissed into her ear, putting his other hand over her mouth. Rosie gasped for breath. She pulled at his arm with her free hand, twisting her head from side to side. His arm moved down to her waist. He lifted her off her feet and slammed her back down, buckling her knees. He instantly covered her nose and mouth again.

He whispered into her ear. "You going to be good? I won't hurt you if you're good."

Rosie tried to nod, struggling to breathe.

"I'm going to take my hand away from your mouth," he said finally. "You don't move, and you don't make any noise."

Rosie nodded energetically, her lungs bursting.

The man took his hand away in increments, testing her promise. Rosie sucked in great drafts of air, but did not cry out. He stood behind her, still twisting her arm. "Good girl. You always were a smart girl."

Rosie's mind raced. Did he know her? She whispered in the smallest voice, "Who are you?"

"It's Roger."

Rosie relaxed just a bit. She spoke very quietly, very controlled. "Let me look at you."

"You'll be good?"

"I promise."

He allowed her to turn to face him, still gripping her arm. His face was newly shaven—the skin whiter, with pink abrasions, over his upper lip. She remembered that he'd had a mustache and heavy sideburns when she saw him at the Convention Center. Now, his hair was plastered back from his forehead with gel. It was dark at the ends, but light brown at the roots.

Her eyes ranged his face. "I can't believe this. You look so much like Daniel."

"Spitting image, wouldn't you say?" He put on thick, black-rimmed glasses which changed him somewhat, but it was still Daniel's face.

Rosie looked down at her arm. "You're hurting me."

"Rosie I have no intentions of doing anything to you. It's just that you hung up on me when I called and I have to talk to you. Can I trust you not to do something stupid?" She nodded and he let her go.

They moved to the kitchen table and sat across from one another. Roger draped his coat over the back of his chair. Rosie rubbed her arm.

"I'm sorry about being so rough," Roger said. "Didn't want you to arouse any neighbors."

She ignored the apology, searching his face. "You're so like Daniel, it's as if you were brothers," she began, still confused.

"Twins, actually," Roger said. "Only I'm the one who got left behind. Danny Boy got adopted out."

Rosie stared at him, bewildered, and he smiled. He seemed to be enjoying having her full attention. "My mom told me about the adoption, that my brother's name was McCallister. At sixteen I ran away from home with a slim hope of finding him. But then I lucked out. Turns out he's part of a prominent family in the city. His dad's the mayor." He smirked the last sentence.

It all sounded like a fantasy, but the physical evidence was right before her eyes. Rosie saw a mixture of jealousy and cruelty in Roger's eyes. He rubbed his upper lip, where his mustache would have been. She recognized the gesture as one Daniel used when he was contemplative.

157

"When we were both seventeen I recognized him in a newspaper photo. He was with his parents."

He tilted his chair back and stretched as if to dissipate his own tension. "So, I've been tracking him for years. I've got a whole scrapbook full of his accomplishments."

"Why?" she asked. "Why did you track him?"

She saw Roger draw back. Clearly there were things he didn't want to say. He struggled with the words. "Early on, when I first ran away, you could say I was in a little trouble. Could have used some help."

Rosie nodded sympathetically to encourage him.

"Well, I wrote him a letter; told him a little about myself."

Rosie hung on every word. "And?"

"And he sent me a thousand dollars and told me to get lost."

"No," Rosie exclaimed. "That can't be. Not Daniel."

Roger's tone was sour. "Yes, your precious Daniel. I've still got the letter."

He went reflective, then brash. "I promised myself I'd send the money back. But I needed it for some new ID, so . . . what the hell."

Rosie shook her head slowly from side to side. This was sounding more and more unbelievable, but she wanted to keep him talking. "Why did you need new ID?"

"I didn't want my old man to find me." His voice told her he wasn't going to elaborate on that.

Rosie sat staring, putting the pieces together. How much of this did Daniel know?

Roger interrupted her thoughts. "Danny Boy's led a charmed life, wouldn't you say?"

"Well, he's always worked hard."

"Worked hard?" He spit the words at her. "A college education, money, socialite wife, yeah, that's really hard work." Roger stopped abruptly as if he regretted his outburst. Rosie said nothing. A few minutes passed.

"So," Rosie ventured when he seemed back in control, "you're blackmailing him."

"Why do you say that?" Roger asked, astonished.

Rosie picked up her purse from the counter. She took out the photo and handed it to Roger.

He looked at it and smiled. "Not a bad likeness." Then he took a closer look. "Hey, isn't this the lobby downstairs?"

"It's not your photo?" she asked.

He chuckled. "No. Kind of wish it were. Who else hates him?"

He tossed the picture on the table. Rosie sat back, her mind racing. If not Roger, then who?

Roger leaned toward her, conspiratorial. "No," he said, "that's not why I'm here. Since that drawing appeared in the paper, connecting him to that Beauchamp case, I've been watching for further developments. Why haven't they charged him?"

Rosie laughed out loud. "With murder? You can't be serious."

Both Roger's palms smacked down on the table. The noise jerked her straight up in her chair. He shouted at her. "I'm dead serious, and don't you forget it! Is our precious Daniel too refined for such an act? Doesn't he ever get his hands dirty? Even with all this shit going on, he still doesn't smell. It makes me sick."

He shoved himself back from the table, scraping the chair on the floor.

Rosie watched him, frightened, wondering where his mood was going. But Roger forced himself to settle down.

Rosie tried for the offensive. "Come on, Roger. How could Daniel possibly be involved?"

"Well you must know Beauchamp was his father."

"That can't be. How do you know?"

"Because he was mine. And a real fine figure of a man he was, too."

Rosie sank backwards. She spoke slowly, things finally falling into place. "Of course, you're the son the police are looking for."

"And they won't find me," Roger boasted. "I've been on the run since I was sixteen and I'm good at it. You didn't recognize me that night at the conference center, did you?"

She gauged his eyes and felt safe enough to ask, "Did you kill him?"

Roger scoffed. "Oh, sure. I'm going to come visit you and talk about a murder I committed. No. I was skiing that week."

Rosie matched his sarcastic tone. "Well, just for drill, why the hell would Daniel do it?"

"I can't believe the cops haven't figured it out. Beauchamp was disgusting. A father like that would be a liability to a rising star like Daniel."

"Daniel just couldn't do that. It's crazy."

Roger thought for a moment. "Maybe not with his own hands. What if someone did him a favor?"

"Like who?"

"Hell, I don't know, but it sure looks to me like someone's protecting him."

They sat for a moment with their own thoughts. Roger's reasoning seemed farfetched to Rosie, but she could see a possible political set up.

Roger picked up the picture from the table. "By the way, when was this taken?"

Rosie said nothing.

Roger mused, "Lots of snow, wasn't real recent." She just stared at him.

Then Roger's face broke into a wide smile. "I'll be damned."

"What?"

"It's automatically dated—down here in the corner."

Rosie knew that. She grabbed the picture out of Roger's hand.

"March 7th," Roger said. He started to laugh, low in his throat at first, then it burst from him in a roar. He rocked back on his chair and threw his hands in the air.

"Roger!" Rosie shouted over his outburst. He seemed out of control. "Roger!"

He quieted, righted his chair and smiled at her, the cat with the canary. His look scared her.

"What's going on?" she asked.

Roger sat for a moment, smiling to himself. He spoke slowly, clearly. "Sorry about that. But when you get the first stroke of luck in your entire life it makes you giddy."

Suddenly Rosie had had enough. She stood. "Look, Roger, I haven't even had my dinner. Tell me why you came here. What do you want from me?"

"Information. I'd like to know what's going on behind the scenes. There's nothing in the news; they must be keeping it quiet. I want to know when he starts sweating."

Rosie wanted to laugh in his face, his stupid theory was so ridiculous. But she decided it was safer not to challenge him any further. "Why do you want to see Daniel charged with murder?" she asked.

"We're brothers, right?"

She nodded. Roger continued, "Except I've been slapped around, kicked and generally pissed on all my life, while darling Daniel has been petted and pampered. I figure he owes me more than a lousy thousand dollars."

"But, his life?" Rosie exclaimed.

"I'll settle for his career."

Roger rose. He put on his coat and moved to the door.

"I could call the police the moment you leave," Rosie said.

Roger turned. "And tell them I impersonated your boss to get into your apartment for a chat?"

"No. Tell them you're the son they're looking for."

Roger's tone was condescending. He spread his hands. "Rosie, Rosie, think. First of all I'd be long gone before they got here. Second, I bet you forgot my last name." He watched her face. Rosie had forgotten, and she knew it showed. "Third, they'll think you're putting down a false scent to get them off your boss's trail. I really doubt they'd believe you."

He opened the door. "I'll be in touch," he said as he left. "And next time, don't slam the phone in my ear."

Rosie sat at the table for a long time, her dinner forgotten. She was eager to know how much of this Daniel knew. If he didn't know about Roger, then she definitely held an ace, and the way things were going she might need one. She decided to leave it up her sleeve.

EIGHTEEN

A stiff wind swept uninhibited across Lake Ontario, a body of water the size of the State of New Jersey. The noon sun reflected off deep, cold blue, and highlighted dancing whitecaps. Holding her jacket collar close against her neck, Sylvia looked up at the imposing Toronto skyline. She'd always liked this city. It had a newer look than most of the eastern cities—clean, fresh and vigorous.

She and Daniel had decided on a walk along the shore for a break from what had been a busy two days, and she was hard-pressed to keep up with his long strides. This was the closest she'd been to happiness in a long time. Daniel continued to make awkward, but sincere, motions at reconciliation. He was terrible at it, but she realized she would eventually have to accept them as payment in full if she wanted to save the marriage.

And even with all their sparring over the last months, there was a steady pull, like a very long rubber band, slowly bringing them back together. They were inching toward intimacy. And when she let herself think about that joining, she felt excitement and anticipation reminiscent of earlier days.

163

She looked up at him. He seemed to be looking far into the distance, his thoughts undoubtedly on his speech. "Thinking about tonight?" she asked.

"You'd think I'd have it down pat by now," he chided himself.

"You do. Every one has gone well."

"But tonight's the big test."

He looked down at her, his eyes full of life. "Jeez, Syl. This is so damned exciting. I'm beginning to think it could actually happen, we could really take the country in a few years."

Sylvia's voice caught in her throat. She took a moment, as if studying the barge moving slowly on the water. "You haven't called me Syl in a long time," she said softly. "It sounds nice."

He slowed his step, then stopped. He turned to face her, putting his hands on her shoulders. His voice resonated with a new kind of respect. "I know that. And I've had to catch myself to keep from saying it. Stupid of me. I've never for one moment stopped loving you, and yet I tried to sound as if it weren't true."

Sylvia studied his eyes, so clear and intense. She wanted so desperately to believe every word. She almost put her arms around him, but hesitated, and lost the moment. They were distracted by shouts and giggles as a bus stopped beside them, disgorging a band of first-graders on a school outing. The eager bodies swarmed around them, each with a yellow placard pinned on, announcing the school's name. Sylvia gently touched the copper-colored hair of a little boy who brushed next to her. As their young teacher tried to herd them into some semblance of order, she caught Sylvia's eye and smiled as if she'd caught two lovers in public.

Slowly the disorganized band formed a small hand-holding army and they marched down the paved path. Sylvia turned to watch them go, her eyes lingering on the little redhead. Somebody's baby. Fear of infertility clutched at her. What if they could never have a child? She felt there was no other way to mend Danny's disappointment. Her shoulders hunched as she covered her face with her hands. Had her abortion been for then, and forever? Had she killed their chances of having more children?

She felt Danny's arms circle her. She leaned into him.

"It's okay," he said, again and again, but she didn't believe it.

NINETEEN

Daniel arrived back in the office on Friday at mid-morning, heady with the success of the trip. He thumped his knuckles on Cathy's desk as he passed and gave her a big smile.

"Things went well?" she teased, knowing the answer.

"The best," he said, thinking, also, of the progress he and Sylvia had made. Not quite there, but so close.

Cathy handed him a manila folder. "I clipped all the news stories. Congratulations."

Daniel took the file, dropped it on his desk, and hung up his coat. He hadn't even sat down before Rosie was in the room, closing the door behind her, looking serious.

"What is it, Rosie?"

She opened an envelope, and placed a photograph on his desk. Daniel picked it up, and his face went white. He tossed it back on the desk as if it were poisonous. He looked across at her, incredulous.

"It came in the mail," she said. "Tuesday."

He slumped into his chair. He rubbed hard at frown lines in his forehead with tense fingers, and squeezed his eyes shut. There were no words to express the disgust he felt at his own foolishness. Daniel looked at the picture on his desk, and saw his career lying there, his marriage lying there. Sylvia seemed about to forgive him in private, but if this became public?

"Let me see the envelope," he said. It was a pathetic, illogical response but he felt he needed to say something. Rosie handed it to him and sat down. He turned it over and over, not believing there was no clue to be found. He got out of his chair. "I've got to find Levy. Know where he is?"

"When he can, he goes to his gym on Fridays at noon," she said.

Daniel found a parking spot a half block from the front of the fitness center. It was the city's finest, bearing a green-veined marble face. He spoke briefly to the pretty young woman at the desk and walked through the expansive weight room. He looked through the glass on the doors to the racquetball courts, and moved toward the showers, self-conscious in his suit. He spotted Levy coming from the steam room, wrapped in a towel.

Barry immediately extended his hand. "Daniel. Welcome back. I heard glowing reports from everywhere on the trip. Congratulations."

Daniel shook his hand briefly and spoke quietly. "We need to get out of here. I need to talk to you."

Levy sobered immediately, his instincts at the ready.

Daniel kept Levy in suspense for five minutes while he drove toward the river, then parked next to the footpath. He dreaded the next moments as he pulled the photo from his pocket and handed it to Levy. Levy studied it. "Where is this?"

"Rosie's apartment building."

Levy opened his mouth and closed it a couple of times. Daniel knew he was trying to control the words he would have liked to shout at him. Levy's eyes pierced sharply into Daniel's face. He spoke as evenly as he could. "Didn't I warn you, you had to be squeaky clean?"

"Yes. I know. But this was just before we had our talk. I had no idea anyone—"

"Could follow you?" Levy asked, not disguising the outrage he felt. "Christ, Daniel."

Daniel looked straight ahead while Levy spoke. "This is dated March 7th. Will there be others?"

"Hell, no. There was only one time."

"If you were caught on your one and only indiscretion, you are the unluckiest goddamned guy walking the earth." His tone said he didn't believe Daniel.

Clearly, the significance of the date hadn't hit Levy. Daniel took a deep breath. "Unfortunately, that was one of the nights the police were questioning me about."

Levy let out an exasperated sigh. "You're telling me that this—" Levy shook the photo in the air between them, his voice rising, "this is your *real* alibi for the night of the murder? Kiss your future goodbye."

Daniel swallowed hard. Suddenly he felt claustrophobic. "Come on, I need to move." He got out of the car.

They walked along the river. It had been gaining momentum, swelling with melting snow along each of the ninety miles it had raced from the mountains, and now rushed past them, noisy.

Levy immediately began analyzing. "You know you're being set up."

"I've thought about it," Daniel said. "The photo, the affair, that's one thing. To tie it in with the murder, that seems a stretch. I think the timing was coincidence."

Levy grunted his disagreement. "When you spent the night with Rosie, who instigated it?"

Daniel remembered her pressing the invitation into his hand. "No one. It just happened."

Levy, reading his hesitation, flared. "Goddammit, Daniel, you'd better start telling me everything and I mean everything if you want me to save your ass. If that's still possible. Now, get your macho ego out of the way, and think. You're sure she didn't orchestrate it?"

"But surely you don't think Rosie . . ." Daniel's voice trailed off.

"Shit," Levy muttered. "Someone got to her."

They walked in silence for a while then Levy summed it up. "So. If this comes down to the wire, either you have no alibi for the night of the murder, or you admit to having an affair." He dropped his voice. "Either way, your career could be finished."

Daniel groped at the only straw he could see. "The other possibility, of course, is that the photo is simple blackmail and we can make it go away."

"We can always hope," Levy muttered. "But I don't think that's it. This thing with Rosie, the timing, it's too neat."

"I'm positive she's innocent," Daniel offered. "She brought me the photo, after all."

169

Levy fixed him with a stare that brooked no argument. "Take her completely out of the loop until we get a handle on this," Levy said. "If it's blackmail we should know pretty quickly."

The roaring of the river reverberated in Daniel's head as they walked. He needed to talk, so he changed the subject. "What about the other son?" He couldn't quite say 'my brother.' "He's got to be my best bet for getting totally clear of this thing. Are they any closer to finding him?"

"I think Greenburg is being straight with me. Unfortunately they've pretty much given that up. For all they know, he could be drinking rum on some beach."

Daniel braced himself for his confrontation with Rosie. She was a quick study, she would no doubt see through him. But he knew Levy was right; she needed to be watched. He took a deep breath, knocked twice and entered her office, closing the door behind him.

She looked up, anxious. "Did you find Levy?"

Daniel nodded. "We think it's probably blackmail. We should know soon."

He cleared his throat. "Rosie, do you have that disk with my weekly schedules on it?"

"Of course."

"Can I have it? Billy is able to give me more hours a week now and I think he could look after the itinerary. Free you up for other things."

Rosie pulled the disk out of her file box. "Let me just make a copy, so I can keep track of you," she said lightly.

Daniel stopped her hand as she started to put it in the computer. "No, I'd rather we just had a single copy around the office."

"But why?" Rosie asked.

"This Beauchamp business has me spooked. Levy thinks I'm being set up. We need to tighten things up a bit."

Rosie handed him the disk. "What's going on, Daniel? You're pushing me out, aren't you?"

"No, Rosie. I want you here. You do a great job. I just want to spread the responsibilities a bit." Daniel knew it sounded phony. He turned and left her office.

That evening, sweats on, Rosie and Cathy sat on either side of a giant bowl of popcorn watching the tango scene from *Scent of a Woman.* Rosie still felt sick to her stomach from Daniel's visit to her office, but Cathy was dewy-eyed, lost in the romance on the screen. When the dance ended she sighed. "I wish more men appreciated women like that, just for their sheer femininity."

"Good luck," Rosie retorted harshly.

"Things getting worse with Daniel?" Cathy asked.

"Rotten." Rosie motioned to the screen. "Mind if I stop this?" Cathy nodded. When the television came back on Rosie muted it.

"I told you the other day I was finished, and I was right. I don't even know why."

"I just can't believe it. Have you had a chance to really talk to him?"

"He's been careful not to give me one," Rosie said. "It's just too hard to talk about in the office."

"Why not force it? Surely, under the right circumstances, he'd be honest with you." Cathy

171

smiled conspiratorially. "I made airline reservations for Sylvia. She's going to Edmonton with a few members of the Junior Symphony early Saturday morning. They're staying overnight."

Rosie sat up, elbows on her knees. Overnight? She smiled inside. A whole evening alone with Daniel. The possibilities were endless. She could regain Daniel's confidence by telling him about Roger. Then, if Roger called her again, and surely he would, she'd plan to meet with him. She and Daniel could set him up. Then Daniel would be put in a position of actually helping the police.

Rosie looked at Cathy with appreciation. "Thanks. I'll try to see him tomorrow night. Can I borrow your car?"

TWENTY

Roger cringed against the ruckus in the crowded unemployment office. Every second person had a hacking cough; snot-nosed children clutched their mothers' legs. His migraine, the second in two days, had him doubled over in the chair. His hair was clownish—light at the roots, orangy, then darker at the ends. An unkempt reddish beard covered his face.

The days since his visit to Rosie's apartment had been spent in self-recrimination. Roger's exultation over the dated photograph vanished when he returned to his apartment that night, empty-handed. Why hadn't he taken it from her? He'd been so overwhelmed by his good fortune he'd not thought properly.

When his name was finally called he was barely able to sit through the degrading interview. A lean woman with a cold voice told him his benefits would cease in a week.

Driving home he kept his eyes closed to slits against the sunlight and entered the apartment building with his head down.

Across the street, Dick Ellis picked up his car phone and dialed. Al answered in his usual curt manner. "Yeah?"

"Hey buddy, it's Ellis. Listen. I'm outside the guy's apartment. This Roger—I've hung around him for a few weekends, but nothing to report. Now I see this other character going in and out of the building, lighter hair, a scruffy reddish beard, but he's got the same glasses and the same kinda walk. And he's driving the Mustang."

"What do you think?" Al asked.

"I think maybe Roger's changing his appearance. This might be fun."

Roger took his pills, crawled into jumbled bed sheets, fully clothed, at four in the afternoon, and slept twelve hours. A thin meowing from under the bed finally woke him. He turned over and rolled his neck, grateful that the headache was gone, and pushed himself up. He sat on the edge of the bed, put on the lamp, and tried to get his mind in gear.

Saturday. Shit. He hated weekends. The papers were full of fun things to do and he pictured everyone else in the world out doing them. He stood, and caught his image in the dresser mirror. He looked like hell. He should shower and shave, but it seemed like too much effort and he sat back down. Mangy scurried out from under the bed to crouch beside the dresser. She looked skinny and Roger couldn't remember when he'd fed her last.

With a defeated sigh, he made himself get up and go out into the living room. He sat down in the pre-dawn dimness and flicked on the TV. It sputtered slowly awake. Clark Gable. Just as Carole Lombard's quirky face came into view it was sucked

174

into a blob and disappeared in the last gasp of the dying TV set. Roger stared at the black square for a few minutes his mind as blank as the screen. Mangy wailed.

He sat for some time just staring into space. All his efforts had been for nothing. In his recent nightmares his mother was unhappy with him. Sometimes she embraced his father and Roger would wake, almost retching at the image. Sometimes she went off with a tall well-dressed man and he would wake with tears in his eyes. And he didn't need dreams to remind him that McCallister was still on his golden rise.

He flicked on the living room lamp and spotted the corner of a red flyer sticking under his door. He got up slowly, opened the door and bent down to retrieve it. Pizza specials. Then Mangy ran between his legs, out into the hallway. He lunged after her, but she dashed away. She was at the end of the hall in seconds, and flying down the stairwell. Roger ran after her, two stairs at a time. A loose piece of carpet tripped him and he went head first down the last six steps. His head smacked against the wall and he jammed his wrist badly, trying to break his fall.

He sat in the shadowy passageway slumped against the handrail, moving the limp wrist back and forth. He felt warm liquid on his forehead. A man shouted from the second floor. "Keep it down. There's people trying to sleep in here." The door slammed.

Roger curled into a fetal ball. From a vast reservoir came giant tears. They streamed down into his beard. He stayed there for a half hour—more alone than the little boy in the warehouse hideout.

After the tears waned, hardness set in. There was nothing left in his life but to get back at McCallister. Consequences were immaterial. He pulled himself to his feet and began to climb up the stairway.

He propped the apartment door open in case Mangy came back. Sitting at the kitchen table, he tried again to write the letter incriminating McCallister, but it wasn't working. There had been a major flaw in his plan. He'd underestimated McCallister's clout. They simply weren't going to touch him.

TWENTY-ONE

Daniel stood in a pool of sunlight in the kitchen of his home, coffee cup in hand. He wished Sylvia were there to share a leisurely Saturday morning, but she'd taken a cab at dawn to get to the airport in time for her flight with the symphony. The house echoed, empty without her. When the phone rang he glanced at his watch wondering if she could be at the hotel so soon.

"Hello," he said hopefully.

A man asked, "Daniel McCallister?" The name came out awkwardly, forced.

"Yes."

There was a pause. Daniel heard labored breathing. Thinking it a prank of some kind, he was about to hang up when he heard, "This is a, friend. An old friend. I thought we might get together."

"Who are you?" Daniel asked.

"I'd rather surprise you."

The voice was unattractive. Threatening? His mind immediately flashed to the photograph of himself in the lobby of Rosie's apartment. Was this his blackmailer? He didn't want to lose him.

"I'm not much good at surprises," he said lightly. "Give me a clue. Old school friends?"

"Farther back. You might say our parents knew each other."

Daniel's breath caught. He didn't speak and there was a long silence as if they were connecting without words.

Finally the other man continued. "Family friends, sort of."

Daniel knew that, at long last, this was his brother. He took a deep breath and spoke as calmly as possible. "Is this Roger?"

Daniel heard a shaky intake of breath.

"That's right. Roger Bollinger."

"Oh, not Beauchamp?" Daniel asked, disappointed.

"No. It's Bollinger now."

Daniel exhaled in relief. "Well, I'm glad you called. I would really like a chance to talk to you." Roger was quiet. Daniel continued slowly, "I've thought of you a lot. Even when I was a child. Where can we meet?"

Roger spoke hesitantly. "I'll pick you up. On a street corner, where I can get a good look around. See that you're alone."

"I'll be alone."

"Fourth Street West and Twelfth Avenue. Southwest corner."

"Fine," Daniel agreed. "What time."

"Eight o'clock tonight."

"I'll be there."

Roger left the apartment at seven forty-five in a state of confusion. McCallister's warm reception had been bothering him all day, softening him. He sat for a few moments in his car, gathering himself for the meeting. He couldn't allow sentimentality to cloud

178

things at this point. His mission was to destroy this man and he would not be deterred. Conjuring up his old jealousy, pumping up his resolve, he started the car.

He didn't notice Dick Ellis' car pull out from the curb.

In anticipation, Daniel arrived at the corner too early and began to feel obvious standing there. He scanned every approaching car, not sure what he was looking for. Himself?

A red Mustang approached. Daniel recognized it from a previous pass. Suddenly the car swerved over to the curb. The driver leaned across the seat and threw the passenger door open, shouting, "Hey, McCallister!"

Daniel jumped in, closed the door, and they sped away.

The air in the car was close, heavy with body sweat. Roger drove fast and erratically. Daniel tried to see what his brother looked like, but the quickly passing street lights gave him only blurred glimpses, and a beard covered most of Roger's face.

Daniel grabbed at the dash as Roger made a sweeping turn, screeching the tires. "Take it easy. There's no one following me," Daniel said.

"You sure?" the other man asked, frowning into his rear-view mirror.

"I'm sure. But keep this up, you'll have the cops on us."

"Yeah, you're right," he said. He hit the brakes.

Dick Ellis swore as Roger slowed too quickly. He was forced to pass them. He made a right turn at the next corner. Making a quick U-turn, he saw them go through the intersection, and was back on the trail.

"Where are we going?" Daniel asked.

"Want to see the old homestead?"

Daniel hesitated, not sure what Roger meant. Then he realized it would be Roger's home. His gut told him this was something he didn't want to do. They drove in silence for about fifteen minutes. Daniel was bursting with questions but sensed that Roger had a need to orchestrate the evening. They passed the fairgrounds—giant buildings looming dark and ominous. Roger jerked his head in that direction. "Worked there once," he said.

"You did?" Daniel said, surprised. For the first time it occurred to him that, in their youth, they might have come close to seeing each other. "Doing what?"

"Running the Ferris wheel, some other rides."

"How old were you then?

"Twenty-five," Roger said, as if embarrassed to admit it.

Daniel was finishing college then. Their lives had been so different, they'd probably never been even close to meeting.

"Have you always lived in the city?" Daniel asked.

Roger shook his head but said nothing more.

As they drove into a neglected part of the city, Daniel's eyes took in the decaying neighborhood with foreboding. They stopped at the curb in front of a small, wooden house. Harsh moonlight showed drapes hung awkwardly; paint peeling from window frames. The front yard consisted of mud puddles interspersed with tufts of brown grass and dog droppings.

Roger swiped the sweat from his upper lip and then his forehead. With nervous movements, he opened his jacket front and rolled down his window. Daniel smelled a fresh burst of body odor.

Roger took a deep breath and turned to Daniel. "Home sweet home," he said.

The ragged edge to Roger's voice made Daniel wince. He looked again at the decrepit building, then back at his brother.

"Is this where you live?" Daniel asked.

Roger snapped to attention. His voice was deafening in the confines of the car. "Shit, no! I wouldn't live in this hell hole. This is *your* home. This is where *you* should be. Don't you understand? This is where you should be."

They stared at one another in the darkness. Having seen the place, Daniel was not surprised at his brother's rage. Nor was he frightened of him, though he could feel Roger struggling to contain his fury. Daniel sat very still, listening to Roger's breathing return to normal. After several minutes Roger sat back in his seat, running his fingers over the steering wheel, seeming to calm himself.

When Daniel felt the time was right he asked, "I'm sorry, I forgot. I'd heard you left home when you were a teenager. Where do you live now?"

"An apartment downtown," Roger muttered. He turned the key in the ignition as if the effort was almost too much. The starter didn't catch immediately and for an instant Daniel feared they would be trapped in front of the home no one wanted to claim.

But the engine turned over.

"Where would you like to go?" Daniel asked. "I'd like us to get out of the car and talk."

"Well, let's go to your place. Mine's kind of crowded."

Roger drove directly to Daniel's house and pulled up the long drive. The interior of the house was dark.

"How'd you know there would be no one else home?" Daniel asked.

Roger looked at Daniel with disdain. The outside lights highlighted Roger's forehead and nose. Daniel saw his first confirmation of their likeness. Roger turned off the engine and grunted. "Too easy. You guys are easier to track than a train. She's in Edmonton with those musicians." He paused, scanning Daniel's face. "You know what? You've got one helluva PR machine. Someone in your family makes the news at least once a week."

"You keep track of us, do you?" Daniel asked.

Roger didn't reply.

They got out of the car and Daniel opened the front door. They entered the house in silence. When Daniel flicked on the lights he had an opportunity to really see his brother. Immediately his heart sank, but he tried to keep the shock out of his eyes. Roger's hair was dirty and wild, his beard ragged and oddly colored. His forehead bore an ugly gash which was caked with dried blood. Seeming to sense the scrutiny, Roger lifted his head and bravely stuck out his chin, but his glasses couldn't hide the despair in the eyes behind them.

"Got a good look?" Roger sneered, moving into the living room. He walked to the fireplace mantel where a half dozen silver-framed photographs stood. He picked one up—an 8x10 of Daniel and Sylvia. Roger studied it and gave a sarcastic 'humph,' setting it back down.

He picked up a picture of Daniel's adoptive parents. "I see no signs of depravity," he pronounced. "Look like decent people."

"I got lucky."

"You don't know the half of it." He put the picture in its place.

"I'd really like to know all of it."

"You couldn't take it," Roger smirked.

"Try me," Daniel said. "I'll get us a drink. Whiskey?"

"No."

Daniel returned with his own drink. "Let's sit." He motioned to two chairs on either side of the fireplace.

After a few minutes Roger spoke, looking around the room. "A stupid quirk of fate put you here and me in hell."

Daniel had no answer for that. He sipped at his drink, then asked, "What are you doing now?"

"Collecting unemployment. Some of your tax dollars at work. I guess I should thank you."

Daniel ignored the remark. "Before that."

Roger leaned forward, cocky, elbows on his knees, ticking items off with his fingers. "Let's see. Dishwasher, pizza delivery, pancake flipper, carnival hawker, ranch hand. Ranch hand means I cleaned the bunkhouse and shoveled shit. Door-to-door salesman. I don't know, I'm missing a few. And, recently, used car sales." He sat back, chin up. "So you can see I'm steadily climbing the corporate ladder."

"Well, at least you've earned your way. More than some can say," Daniel put in.

Roger's eyes narrowed and he spit out the words. "Don't patronize me."

183

"Sorry. Can you tell me about before that? Your childhood?"

Roger shook his head. "No."

Daniel took a drink. "Well, you called me. What do you want to talk about?"

Roger looked at him squarely. "The end of your career."

Daniel was taken aback by Roger's voice as much as by his words. There was no uncertainty there. Daniel stood, to gain the advantage. "You want to ruin me? Why? What did I ever do to you?"

Roger stood as well, very close. He stared into Daniel's eyes, leaning forward. His entire demeanor changed into one of a predator. "You left me," he whispered. Roger's breathing became heavy, his hands moved nervously up and down the front of his jacket. Suddenly he smacked the mantel with a flat palm, a sound almost as sharp as a gunshot. Roger yelled into Daniel's face, "You abandoned me!"

Daniel stood very still; there was a hint of craziness here. They stared at each other, Roger blinking first. Daniel spoke quietly. "No. You've got it wrong. Our mother left me."

"Our mother? Our mother?" Roger screamed. He swept his arm across the mantel. Photos crashed to the floor. Daniel swallowed involuntarily.

Roger began to pace the room, flinging his arms wildly. "Funny, I didn't see you at the funeral. I didn't see you at the hospital. You didn't come when he beat her up."

"I would have come," Daniel said, quietly. "I didn't know where you were."

Daniel thought he heard a strangled sob and saw Roger's shoulders slump. But in a moment Roger's voice snapped at him again. "Yeah, well some of us don't constantly advertise our whereabouts."

Daniel allowed a few more minutes of Roger's pacing. He drained his glass and put it on the coffee table.

"Did you kill our father?" he asked.

Roger didn't hesitate. "I did it for her. He deserved it."

"I'm sure he did," Daniel said. "I know about the abuse."

Roger turned toward him, warning him off the subject with a black scowl.

Daniel changed course. "It looks like the perfect murder. My guess is you knew the police would eventually come after me. Did you plan for me to take the fall?"

"Hell, yes. I want to ruin you, even the score a bit. So far money has protected you. Well that's about to change. The cops are going to work you over good."

"Why wouldn't I simply point them in your direction?"

The first hint of a smile crossed Roger's face. "Because only one of us has an alibi." He paused as if to let that sink in. "That photograph of you at Rosie's place? The cops will love that; it's dated you know."

Daniel's teeth clenched. "You know Rosie?"

"Oh, yeah. We go 'way back," Roger taunted. "I'm shocked she hasn't mentioned me."

Daniel paced a few steps. He'd only seen a miserable and pathetic man, when in reality there was significant danger here. Was Levy right? Was Rosie involved? Were the two of them setting him up? But what could Rosie gain? "So," he said slowly, gathering his thoughts, "you didn't need to meet with me tonight. You could simply send the picture to the police, if you have it. What do you want, money?"

Roger's jaw dropped like a brick. At first he seemed dumbstruck. Then he shouted, his voice incredulous, "Money? It's always money with you." His hands flew into the air, he began to pace the room again.

"What do you mean, it's always money with me?"

Roger spun around. "It wasn't the damned thousand dollars that kept me away all this time."

Daniel searched Roger's face. "What thousand dollars?"

Roger reached into his back pants pocket and pulled out his wallet. He dug out a piece of paper, folded several times and smashed flat by being tucked into its tiny home for so long. He threw the letter at Daniel's feet. Daniel picked it up, carefully unfolding the frayed corners. He recognized his father's handwriting immediately. He looked at the date and saw that it was written years ago, while he and his mother were in Europe. He read it and felt ill. His father had bribed Roger to stay out of their lives. What had his father intended? To protect Daniel, or himself?

Daniel looked over at Roger. "I've never seen this before. Believe me. My father must have written it. This makes me sick," he murmured. He half-heartedly handed it back.

Roger pushed it away. "Yeah, well, it made me sick, too."

Then Roger began to strut, taking command. "No, I didn't come for more money." He walked over to the baby grand and slammed both fists down on the keyboard. A discordant crash of notes filled the room. Leaning on the piano he turned to Daniel and spoke softly. "No. I don't want money. I want this piano."

He moved over to the silk sofa, tracing his fingers along its elegant spine. He whispered, "I want this couch." He bent and picked up the photo of Daniel and Sylvia from the floor. He held it out toward Daniel. His voice began to rise. "I want this blonde." He seemed frustrated by Daniel's immobility and screamed into Daniel's face. "Don't you see? I want this fucking life!" He flung the framed photo with all his might. It crashed into the leaded window, taking out one of the small panes. He grabbed the fireplace poker and swung it in a wild arc. Daniel had barely enough time to react as the iron bar narrowly missed his head. In a frenzy, Roger thrashed about with the poker. The silk of the sofa split easily, spilling its innards. The poker gouged at the baby grand. Daniel lunged and got him in a bear hug from behind, struggling to keep the damage to a minimum. But the strength of anguish fueled Roger. He escaped Daniel's grasp time and again, dashing lamps and precious vases to the floor, overturning ornate tables, all the while moaning.

The shattering of the window brought Dick Ellis to full attention. He had been half dozing, waiting for Roger to come out of the house. The beveled, leaded windows distorted his view but he could see that there was a terrible struggle going on. He picked up his phone, keeping one eye on the action.

"Al? Hi, it's Dick. Listen, this Roger guy I'm tailing . . . he picks up a guy on the street, they drive around, then end up at this fancy house. Now they're try'na kill each other."

"You get out of there," Al said. "Gimme the address. I'm calling the cops. I'm gonna nail his skinny ass."

Daniel could feel Roger weakening. The poison was flowing from him, depleting him. He wrapped his arms around Roger's middle from behind and flung his brother sideways with all his strength. Roger fell heavily, his head striking the piano leg. He lay still as a corpse. Daniel bent over him, listening for breath.

A yellow light, followed by a blue tinge, streaked across the wall. Daniel jumped up and ran to the window. A police car, strobe lights turning, approached the house. He flicked off the living room light.

"That light just went out," the junior officer announced as his partner slowed the car.

"Can you see the address?" Jim Proctor asked.

· The younger man put his high-powered flashlight on the front door. "Yeah, this is it."

The two of them moved up the long walkway, glancing into the shadows on either side of the hedges. Jim Proctor pushed the doorbell. They could hear it chime inside. Proctor banged on the door with his fist. They couldn't hear or see any movement.

Proctor banged again. "Police!" he barked. "Is everything all right in there?" They heard footsteps. After a moment the door opened slowly. Proctor saw a dishevelled man, tucking a torn shirt into his trousers. He was breathing heavily.

"Sorry to keep you," the man said. "I was just upstairs getting ready for bed."

"We've had a report of some violence," Proctor said.

"Yes," he said. "I had a visitor. There was a tussle, but everything is all right now."

"Nobody hurt?"

"No. No one's hurt."

"This your home?"

"Yes."

"Can I see some identification?"

The man pulled his wallet from his back pocket, opened it to his driver's license and handed it over. The officer gave it a quick look and handed it back. "Mind if we take a look inside?"

Daniel hesitated only momentarily; this was no time to antagonize the police. He stepped backwards, allowing the policemen further into the foyer. He reached behind them and closed the door. The hallway light allowed them to see into the living room.

"Where is your visitor?" the first officer asked, more interested now.

"He left a few minutes ago."

"Do you mind if we have a look around?"

"Not at all."

"Your visitor, does he have a weapon?"

Daniel shook his head, no. The officer jerked his thumb in the direction of the back door. "Randy, check outside," he said. Then he walked into the living room, putting on the light. "This looks like a lot more than a tussle."

"Well, it looks worse than it was," Daniel explained.

As the policeman observed the debris, Daniel forced his own eyes away from the piano. Was there blood on the leg where Roger's head had hit?

The second officer returned through the back door. "No one outside. Back door was unlocked."

The older officer jerked his thumb toward the driveway, speaking to Daniel. "That your car out there?"

"No. That's his," Daniel said.

"He left without his car?" He gave Daniel a withering look. "Who is he?"

Daniel had to blink twice before his memory kicked in. "Roger Bollinger," he said flatly.

"A friend? Business acquaintance, what?"

"It was a family thing."

The officer made a few notes. "You want to press charges?"

"Oh, definitely not. No. I appreciate your concern, but, really everything's all right."

Daniel sat down, his head in his hands, attempting to evade any more questions. He could sense they hated to let it go.

"You're sure you don't want us to stick around. He'll be back for his car."

Daniel stood, moving them toward the door. "No. Thank you." He tried to give them a reassuring smile. "We've settled everything."

"Well, do it more sensibly next time," the first officer cracked as they departed.

As Proctor pulled the police car from the curb Randy said, "Surely he wouldn't go without his car. Let's do a quick spotlight search in the area, maybe we'll see him."

Rosie struggled to get Cathy's old Dodge into first gear as the light turned green. She wished she'd taken a cab. After a terrible grinding noise the gear settled into place and the car lunged forward. Rosie turned into Daniel's neighborhood, admiring the large, elegant homes. She rehearsed her upcoming conversation with her boss. Roger was her ticket back into Daniel's good graces, and Daniel would be very appreciative. It should be easy to translate that into deepening their personal relationship. She smiled at the thought of one day living in a neighborhood like this.

As she approached Daniel's address she saw a police car pulling slowly away from the curb. It was crawling along, making a sweeping search with a strong light. She passed the car, and the small park farther down the road, then made a left turn. What could be the problem? She decided to circle the neighborhood for a few minutes, then go back to Daniel's house.

TWENTY-TWO

Sam Fisher, a runner, hated exercising indoors, and this winter had forced him to breathe far too much recycled air. The sun had not fully risen, and already the exposed skin on his face and legs glistened with a hint of sweat. Across the river from where he ran, the heart of the city was not yet beating. Sam felt that the sweetness in the air, and the reaching arms of the naked trees, and the roar of the river were his alone.

He always ran the same six-mile loop that started on the streets and ended with a stretch through the park. The path along the river swirled with a foot of muddy water. Sam picked his way just out of the water's reach, enjoying the need to jump puddles and plan ahead in order to keep his speed up.

When it was time for a cool-down, Sam slowed to a brisk walk, his lungs pumping. He was hot and the air felt bracing as it found all the damp spots. The sun was in his eyes now; he turned them downward to escape the glare. Otherwise he might never have seen the body tangled in the swirling debris. It turned slowly in an eddy, threatening to break loose and join the rush of the main flow.

Sam ran into the water. It was up to his knees and pulling at him by the time he could reach an out-flung arm. He flinched at the plastic feel of the cold hand and grabbed instead the jacket sleeve. He made slow progress pulling backwards, having to remove, with his free hand, sticks and pieces of bushes that were clawing at the man's clothing. The icy water made his hands and feet ache and twice he almost lost his grip.

Finally, with the body resting on firm land, Sam looked at the face. He was no medical expert, but was sure the person was dead. And Sam was just as sure he'd died in agony; the man's haggard face registered desperation.

A half-hour later a policeman pulled a soggy wallet from the victim's pants pocket. It was old, cracked leather, but it had been folded over twice, and was crammed tightly into the pocket, protecting the contents pretty well. "Roger Bollinger," he read from the driver's license, "#204, Klondike Building, 801 Tenth Avenue." Another officer was dispatched to Roger's address to notify any family.

When the landlord opened the door to Roger's apartment, both men jerked back from the stench of sour food and dirty cat litter. The kitchen floor was ankle-deep in torn, discarded newspapers and balled-up writing paper. The officer picked an unfinished letter from the table. It accused a Daniel McCallister of lying about his alibi the night of the Beauchamp murder. He called his sergeant.

Sunday morning had started well for Detective Sullivan. He woke to the smell of fresh coffee. His wife, Muriel, was standing by the bed with a cup in her hand. She was wrapped in his heavy robe, the top of which fell open when she bent over and kissed him. He reached into the warm folds of the velour and caressed her full breasts.

Muriel put the coffee cup on the side table. He held the comforter up in a tent and she rolled inside. Sullivan smiled to himself. Who'd have thought his sex life would still be this good at this time of life? Not that it happened often. But it happened when least expected, and after lengthy dry periods, which made it all the more exciting. Last night had been such a night.

He pulled her close.

When the phone rang Sullivan groaned aloud. When he recognized Chief Greenburg's voice he hoisted himself on one elbow and paid attention.

Sullivan shook his head as Greenburg recounted the details. "Looked like a simple drowning. But, from what we found in his apartment, this guy was apparently ready to finger McCallister for the Beauchamp murder. Of course our first reaction was to talk to McCallister, but then I'm told a couple of officers were talking to him—just last night."

Sullivan sat up straighter and straighter as he listened. Greenburg recited McCallister's fight with his visitor—a Roger Bollinger.

Sullivan, naked, paced beside the bed.

As the Chief finished the story he moaned. "I sure didn't want it to be this way, but it looks bad. I want you and Duke to talk to the coroner, then the officers who saw McCallister last night. Do what you have to do."

The coroner was preparing to undress the body as Sullivan and Duke entered the room. The partners studied the face. The beard and hair were twisted and matted with mud and debris. They stood staring at it.

"He looks like a rummy. What could be the connection?" Sullivan mumbled to Duke. "Why was this guy blackmailing McCallister?"

Sullivan's gaze kept going back to the area around the eyes and nose. He turned to Duke. "This face seem familiar at all?"

"Huh, uh." Duke shrugged.

Sullivan turned to the coroner. "Let me know as soon as you have the report." His gaze lingered on the face.

Duke was checking Bollinger's effects. The wallet contained two one-dollar bills, a driver's license and a picture of a woman not far beyond her teenage years. She was pretty, and at first glance the detective thought it was the man's girlfriend. Except that the photo was in black and white and it was old and soft at the edges from handling. Duke pulled it carefully from its slip. He turned it over and read aloud. "Maryanne Scott, 1958."

Duke's mouth dropped open. He looked at Sullivan in disbelief. "I'll be goddamned!" he said. "It's the brother."

"What brother?" Sullivan snapped, impatient with his partner's loud enthusiasm so early in the day.

"Maryanne Scott was Roger's, and McCallister's, mother. The reason he looks familiar to you is this guy is Roger Beauchamp." Duke rubbed his hands together. "Damn," he said, grinning, "I knew there was something connecting McCallister to the Beauchamp murder."

Sullivan sat down heavily on a wooden chair. "Shit," he muttered.

Duke paced. "So, McCallister did the murder, his brother knew it, and came to the house trying to blackmail him."

He looked to Sullivan for confirmation, but got none.

Duke continued, "They fought, and McCallister silenced him."

Sullivan held up a hand to stop him. "Easy, Mike. So far all we've got is speculation. And it just doesn't feel right. McCallister's far too savvy to get involved in an unnecessary killing."

"Well the brother obviously knew something. So the second one *was* necessary."

"Okay. Maybe I can buy that. It sure looks like he did his brother in, but we have no more to go on on the first murder than we had before." Sullivan sighed and hoisted his body upward. "But we're walking on eggs here. A false arrest and we'll be on the street, and I don't mean walking a beat."

TWENTY-THREE

The newspaper, wrong as usual, had said the entire junior orchestra was making the trip to Edmonton, when, in fact, only a few of the very best musicians were invited to the regional scholarship finals. Sylvia found that being in charge of just four of the youngsters kept her busy. The dozen competitors, their parents and a few volunteers had arrived in Edmonton Saturday morning. In the afternoon the children practiced, parents worried, and Sylvia helped make last minute corrections to Sunday's program and took it to the printer. In the early evening she called Daniel, disappointed at not finding him home. Momentary doubts flashed across her mind as to where he might be, but she pushed them aside and decided not to call again as if checking up on him. A new start meant new faith.

The judging started early Sunday morning, Sal White among the first contestants. Sylvia crossed her fingers. She remembered how his dark eyes had sparkled when she took the gleaming violin from its case and handed it to him—a gift made possible by her father's contribution.

"For me?" He was amazed.

"Yes, Sal. It's yours. You'll make it sound like the voices of angels."

He reached out tentatively and she laid it across his arms. "Thank you, Mrs. McCallister," he said, already tucking it under his chin, testing the fit. He stepped back from her and drew the bow across the strings in a slow arpeggio. His face lit up when he heard its full timbre.

"It's beautiful," he whispered.

Now, in the huge concert hall, his young face scrunched in concentration, he was making his new violin sing. There was utter quiet among the audience—they knew they were listening to a future star.

As she watched Sal, Sylvia allowed herself, for the very first time, to wonder what the baby she had aborted might have become, had it been given life. Her defense against guilt and depression had always been to put such thoughts from her mind. Would she and Danny now be watching a son or daughter on such a stage, or maybe on a football field? Were these the kinds of things Danny imagined, in his obsession over the lost child? Suddenly Sylvia only wanted to be home with him, telling him she understood some of his pain.

She searched out one of the other chaperons and asked her to take on the extra responsibilities, then returned to the hotel, packed quickly and caught a commuter flight.

Two hours later her cab approached the front of the house. "That's a long driveway," the cabbie remarked. "Shall I pull up?"

Sylvia hesitated because she saw an old red Mustang parked in the driveway and a broken window pane in the living room with a slab of electrician's tape across it. "No," she said, paying him at the curb. Leaving her bag on the sidewalk, she ran to the front door.

"Danny? Are you here?" she called as she entered.

"In here, Syl," a sad voice said from the living room.

Sylvia looked through the doorway. Her mind could barely take it all in. A broom was propped against the wall, in a pile of broken glass. Some lamps stood without their shades. Some were shattered. The pictures on the wall tilted crazily. The mantel was piled with broken picture frames and the silk sash that had lain across the piano lay, ripped, underneath it. And Danny sat in the midst of the devastation, on the tortured sofa, his back to her.

He turned his head slowly in her direction. He patted the seat beside him. "Come," he said simply.

"My God, Danny," she began, as she got a full look at him. He was unshaven, his shirt torn and smudged, his hair matted with sweat. She took both his hands. "Are you all right?"

"My brother came to see me last night." He waved one arm to encompass the room. "You can see we're really quite close." Then his eyebrows came together and he winced.

Sylvia squeezed his hand. "Tell me," she said softly.

Daniel recounted Roger's phone call, their visit to the Beauchamp house, and the struggle. His voice died away. Stunned at the destruction of her home, Sylvia got up and moved among the ruins. She traced her finger over a deep, raw gouge in the piano. "But why ruin beautiful things?" she asked.

199

"You can't fathom the depth of his hatred," Daniel answered. "His entire life must be sheer hell. God, Syl, you should have seen him. Dirty, scraggly, utterly beaten down. He wanted to ruin me completely. And, somehow, he knows Rosie."

Sylvia walked slowly to the window trying to grasp the consequences of these statements.

"Where is he now?"

Daniel put his head in his hands and moaned. "He'd told me about killing our father, which would have cleared me, but I couldn't turn him over. When the police showed up I panicked—"

She spun around. "Why were the police here?"

"I don't know. Maybe a neighbor called them because of the fight." He rose on shaky legs and walked toward her. Sylvia hugged him and felt his full weight slump against her. "I was so excited, waiting to meet him, but he truly hated me."

The door chime startled them both. Sylvia pulled away from Daniel. She opened the door to Detective Sullivan. A younger officer stood slightly behind him. Sullivan handed her the suitcase she'd left on the sidewalk.

"Hello, Detective Sullivan," she said, a question in her voice. She felt Daniel at her side.

"Mrs. McCallister," he acknowledged, his voice sober. "May we come in?"

"Of course." She and Daniel stepped back.

Sullivan made a curt introduction of Detective Michael Duke, then spoke quickly and firmly to Daniel. "We'd like you to come down to the station and answer some questions about your visitor last night."

"Why?"

"Roger Beauchamp is dead."

"He's dead?" Sylvia exclaimed. She spun around and looked at Daniel. His hands covered his face and his head dropped. "Danny?"

"Oh, dear God," he said.

Daniel moved like an old man in the direction of the door. Sylvia gripped his arm to hold him back. "He's been up all night," she said to Sullivan. "Couldn't he do this later, after he's had a chance to rest and clean up?"

Daniel turned to her, an incredible sadness in his face. "It's okay Syl. I'd as soon get it over with." He moved out of her hold.

"I'm calling Barry right now."

Daniel stopped. His eyes connected with hers and he seemed to come to his senses. "Yes, call Barry."

TWENTY-FOUR

Barry Levy's Mercedes came to a screeching halt in the police station parking area. He quickly cleared his identification with the officer on the desk and sprinted to the room where Daniel waited. Barry and his wife had returned from a weekend retreat late Sunday afternoon to find a half dozen messages from Sylvia, each one more anxious than the last.

"Where the hell have you been?" Daniel demanded, jumping up.

Barry put a finger to his mouth and Daniel shut up.

When they were settled in a completely private room, Levy said, "I stopped by Chief Greenburg's house. Your dad was there, badgering him, but the Chief didn't waver. They have some pretty serious suspicions. Now tell me everything that happened."

Levy studied Daniel's face intently as he told the whole story, up to the police picking him up today.

"Who alerted the police last night?" was Barry's first question.

Daniel shrugged. "I assumed it was some neighbor. Perhaps someone was outside when the window shattered. I'd neglected to pull the drapes."

Levy nodded. "So when the police car pulled up they could see in?"

"I saw them coming and switched off the lights."

"Great. What every innocent person does when he sees the police."

Daniel looked at the floor. "I know, it was stupid, a gut reaction."

"We can walk out of here right now unless they charge you, and I think they'd have done that already if they were going to."

"Won't leaving now make me look more suspect?"

"Makes no difference."

"I'd as soon get it over with," Daniel said. "I've got nothing to hide."

"Fine. But let's go over everything one more time."

The room where Sullivan met them was about ten by twenty, cool and drab. He sat at an aged, yellowed, pine slab table, ringed around the edges with gray finger marks. Sullivan motioned Daniel and Levy to their chairs and made it clear that he was flipping on the tape recorder. Sullivan's questioning was precise and monotonous, every detail of the conversation with Roger and the struggle dissected again and again.

"Let's start again—at the point where you flick off the living room light," Sullivan said.

Daniel groaned. He was as exhausted as he'd ever been in his life.

Levy glared at Sullivan. "Only one more time. Then we're out of here."

Daniel began reciting. "Roger was lying on the floor. He moaned, so I knew he was conscious. I grabbed him by the jacket and hauled him to his feet. He faltered, but I half dragged him down the hall to the back door. His feet were finally under him when I shoved him outside."

Sullivan ended on an incredulous note. "This was the man who might be able to shed some light on your father's murder, and you let him go?"

Daniel didn't answer.

Sullivan's tone changed to aggression. "You knew that he was your brother. Why did you lie to the police officers when they asked who your visitor was?"

"I didn't. I only told them his name was Roger Bollinger, which it is . . . was." Daniel slumped, his head in his hands.

The sound of Sullivan picking up a piece of paper made him look up. It was the paper from Roger's apartment—wrinkled, with his brother's handwriting on it. He'd read it aloud twice already. Daniel felt tears threatening and his head fell into his hands again. "Is there any credence to this claim, that he could destroy your alibi for the night of the murder?"

Levy reached to place a cautionary hand on Daniel's arm, too late.

With his head down, Daniel nodded.

Levy jumped to his feet. "A moment with my client," he said, all but pulling Daniel out of his chair.

"I'll get a coffee," Sullivan muttered, glaring at them both. He switched off the recorder.

When the door closed Levy hissed at Daniel through gritted teeth, "You fool! You pay me for advice. Why don't you take it?"

Daniel backed away from the onslaught. He ran both hands up over his hair, pulling it harshly back from his forehead. "Christ, Barry, I'm so damned tired. I'm sorry. There's nothing on the tape, though."

Levy shook his head in disgust. He made a gargantuan effort to control his voice. "Look, they think you beat him up, dragged him to the river and threw him in."

"In a way, I did."

"Shit, Daniel. Get a grip. You're beat up yourself, and tired, and not thinking straight."

Sullivan knocked and opened the door a crack.

"Come in," Levy said. "My client has nothing more to say at this point. Charge him, or let him go."

Sullivan returned to his chair, assessing them both. The Chief had made it clear that this was his call. Sullivan was disappointed in Daniel. His hunch from the beginning was Daniel's innocence and he hated to think his intuition was going, along with his hair. But McCallister had lied to the officers. The police had seen McCallister turn off the interior lights when they pulled up. What was he hiding? And when Sullivan and Duke went back to the house for a further look they found the years-old letter telling Roger, essentially, to get lost. McCallister's story, that it was written by his father, was weak; they'd have to check the handwriting and maybe the European travel story. McCallister could well have known about the brother all along.

But what would a good defense lawyer do with these 'facts'? And Sullivan knew McCallister would be hiring the best. The police had some hard investigating ahead of them before they could make an arrest that would stick.

He waved his hand toward Daniel. "Don't take any vacations."

Levy drove in silence until he pulled into the McCallister driveway. "It'll be okay," he said. He seemed to want to reach out and touch Daniel, but could not. "If the worst happens, and they charge you, I've already got Jimmy McIntosh apprised. He's in Vancouver, the best defense attorney in the country. But it's just a precaution. It won't happen."

"Thanks, Barry," Daniel called back, as he started toward the house.

As soon as he opened the door Sylvia was in his arms. She hugged him fiercely, and he could feel her heart pounding. As she pulled back to search his face, he saw a new tautness in the skin around her eyes, the pull of worry.

"Are you all right?" she asked, running her hand over the harsh beard, smoothing his hair. He nodded, holding her tightly again.

They sat at the kitchen table through an early dinner and for two hours afterward. Daniel was beyond tired, his mind unable to shut down. The conversation moved back and forth between the trauma he felt over Roger's death and the stark reality of a possible murder charge.

"My career is probably shattered. That's what he wanted. That's all he wanted."

"I don't believe that's all he wanted," Sylvia countered. "He didn't have to come to the house. He wanted to see you. If the police hadn't shown up you two might have come to some . . . I don't know, some kind of peace."

"I'd like to think so." He reached across the table and took her hand. "Let's go to bed."

Sylvia dressed in a silk white negligee with the slimmest of straps. When she came out of the dressing room she sat on the bed watching Daniel. She wanted to distract him, but was not having much success. He stood, hands locked behind him, staring out over the back yard, the rock wall, and the river.

"Danny, come away," she said. "Why torture yourself?"

He spoke quietly. "I always knew there was someone missing from my life. I always felt that pervading loneliness." He half turned and looked back at her. "I must have had some innate knowledge. I think that terrible sense of loss from years before is what made me react so strongly about the abortion. I know you did what you thought was right at the time, for both of us."

She looked up at him. "Thank you Danny. I've needed to hear that."

He pulled her to her feet. She loosened his robe and ran her hands over his chest. He wrapped his arms around her, crushing their bodies together, his mouth covering hers. His mind went numb, racing away from every care, every thought of the last months.

Marlene Baird

TWENTY-FIVE

Detective Sullivan snapped open the Monday morning paper. The reporter had savaged McCallister. Sullivan would have liked to get his hands on the police officer who talked this time. There was always some little nobody who wanted a moment in the sun, or a few dollars.

"MAJORITY PARTY LEADER McCALLISTER QUESTIONED IN MURDER CASE" emblazoned the front page. The piece was so slanted that the average reader would be expecting a murder charge at any minute. And McCallister was accused of turning his back on his 'real' family, the miserable Beauchamps, in a futile attempt to save his political hide. They had dug up the computer drawing of Roger's face and run it beside a photo of Daniel. They spared no gore in describing Roger's beaten body, found near the bridge, drowned. They gave the public another dose of the ugly 'snowman' murder, letting their imaginations take them wherever.

Sullivan folded the paper impatiently and stuck it under his desk as a sixtyish man hobbled toward him.

"Detective Sullivan?" the man asked.

208

Sullivan nodded. This must be the guy who'd called. Said he had information about Saturday night. They'd spoken briefly on the phone, then Sullivan asked if he could come down and make a statement. Sullivan motioned him to sit.

Dick Ellis struggled to get his swollen leg comfortable. The chair was too close to the detective's desk and there was no room to shift back. In the end he turned his chair and let the leg stick out into the aisle.

"Thank you for coming forward, Mr. Ellis," Sullivan said.

Ellis felt a chill between them. He guessed there was not a policeman alive who liked private investigators—until they were one.

"Yeah, well, once I saw in the paper how things were stackin' up, I figured I'd better."

Sullivan leaned across the desk. "Now, you said on the phone that you recognized the address in the news story as the house you'd been watching."

Ellis nodded.

"Why were you watching that house?"

"I was tailin' this guy, Roger. His ex-boss had a grudge. Al, that's my client, thought Roger had slashed the tires on his car lot."

Sullivan grunted. "What did you see at the house that alerted you?"

"Something crashed into the window, bustin' it. That got my attention. When I see the fight goin' on I call my client and he tells me to get out of there. He says he's gonna call the cops."

"But you didn't actually leave the area, even after the police arrived."

"No. Curious. Nature of the beast, eh?" Ellis said lightly. Sullivan didn't respond.

Ellis cleared his throat and continued. "I move on down the street, turn around to face the direction of the house and park in front of the residences on the other side of the street. I see the cops arrive at McCallister's house."

"How far away were you?"

"Oh, ah, two houses down from McCallister's is where the park starts. I'm maybe a couple hundred yards into the park area, but across the street."

Sullivan was sketching a diagram. He nodded. "Go on."

"Well, I sit while the cops are in the house. After about ten minutes they come out. They drive slowly at first, flashing the spot between the houses. Seem to be looking for someone, but not too hard, then they take off."

"They didn't see you?"

Ellis shook his head. "I dropped under the dash."

Sullivan pursed his lips. "Then?"

"Well I'd really jammed my bad leg getting down, so I sit for a few minutes letting it ease up. Then a car comes cruising slow. It had just passed that way a bit earlier; I remember because it was an old eighty-two Dodge. Used to have one just like it."

Sullivan stared at him, not hiding his impatience.

"A girl was in it," Ellis said.

"Did she see you?"

"Huh-uh. She's too busy looking back at the house, until something catches her eye in the park."

"How do you know? Wasn't it dark?"

"There was some light from the park lamps so she was sort of in profile, know what I mean?"

Sullivan nodded. "And?" he asked.

"She stops across the street from me, not directly. She gets out, on the passenger side, stands in the light of her open car door, takes a real good look around. I crouch down again. She turns in my direction, seems to be studying the houses behind me, then looks back toward the park."

"Could you identify her?"

"I doubt it. She was slim, with a mop of hair, but lots of girls have that. And she was over on the other side of her car, away from me."

He shifted his leg with both hands. The pain made him grunt.

"Then she cups her hands to her mouth and starts yellin', 'Daniel, Daniel.'"

Sullivan's eyebrows shot up and Ellis smiled inside.

"Then she starts running into the park. I automatically open my car door, just habit, I wanted to follow. But this stopped me." He patted his thigh.

Sullivan waited for more.

"So, I wait for a good five minutes, cursing my damn leg. I'm curious as hell. Then here she comes, fast, back to the car. Jumps in and takes off."

"Did you follow her?"

Ellis shook his head. "My wife had called me on the car phone. She needed me at home. She's not well."

Sullivan sighed like the ceiling had come down and squashed him. "But you had plenty of time to get the plate, right?"

With a grunt, Ellis pulled a slip of paper from his pocket and tossed it on Sullivan's desk. "Yeah, I got the plate. Only a moron would have missed that."

Cathy hunched low in the big chair, wishing she'd toughed out her head cold and gone in to work. But the news about Daniel had shaken her completely and she really didn't want to be answering anyone's questions. She sure never expected to be answering the ones that had been coming from the two men facing her.

She pulled the heavy chenille robe close around her neck and pushed at her stringy hair. Then her hand found the hole in the upholstery on the side of the cushion. She nervously rubbed at it.

The younger detective, Duke was his name, seemed sympathetic, but the other one was definitely in charge. When they arrived at the door she thought they were canvassing for a church group, dressed so formally. She'd never seen detectives before. She'd already forgotten the older one's name.

At first she was thoroughly confused and they were pretty harsh with her, wanting to know where she was Saturday night and not believing her when she said she was at home. They asked about her car, and she explained about loaning the car to Rosie. Since then things had gone better.

Finally, they seemed about to leave.

She screwed up her courage. "What do you want Rosie for? She couldn't have done anything."

The nice one said, "Probably not. We just want to ask her a couple of questions. When did she bring the car back?"

"Sunday afternoon."

They both stood, towering over her. "Do you have her address?" the older man asked.

She recited it for him. "But she'd be at the office now. She works for Mr. McCallister, too."

The moment they left, Cathy picked up the phone and dialed Rosie's private number.

"It's Cathy. How are things going down there?"

"It's horrible. I called the temporary agency and put a girl at your desk just to field calls. At least she can honestly say she knows nothing. How are you feeling?"

"Awful. I just had two detectives here."

"Detectives? At your house?" Cathy heard panic in Rosie's voice.

"They were asking about Saturday night. About where my car was."

"Damn!" Rosie said. There was a moment of quiet.

"Rosie?" Cathy asked.

"Look, Cathy, I've got a lot going on here. Let me call you back." The line went dead.

Rosie swore under her breath as she pulled a few personal items from her desk and stuffed them into her briefcase. If someone had seen the car, why hadn't she seen that person? What else had the person seen? She quickly scribbled a note and took it into Daniel's office. She forced herself to take long, even breaths as she put on her coat.

She walked calmly out to the reception area and told the temp at Cathy's desk she had an appointment and would be back in an hour.

Her personal bank was only two doors down the street. She withdrew the bulk of her two-thousand dollar savings account. In the restroom of a nearby restaurant she scrubbed off her makeup and pulled her hair into a severe roll, but it didn't make her look that different. She ran across the street to a bargain department store. All but racing down the aisles, she grabbed up beige polyester pull-on pants, a squared off white cotton blouse that would hang shapelessly below the waistline, a gaudy green sweater and some plastic earrings. She grabbed a nylon duffle bag. Rosie grimaced as she picked up cheap shoes, and pulled a loose-fitting coat from the rack. From a pile of miscellaneous winter mark-downs she took a wool hat that would accommodate all her hair, and a black imitation alligator purse.

She changed in the restroom of another restaurant, stuffing her good clothes and her briefcase into the duffle bag.

The apartment manager at Rosie's building spruced right up when he saw the badges and the search warrant. Typical, Sullivan thought, makes his day. A small man with dark eyes set too close together, he unlocked her door with a ferret-like conspiratorial grin.

"What you looking for?" he asked.

Sullivan stared him down.

Duke went directly for the bedroom and opened the closet. There were no major gaps in the clothes. He pushed to the back and saw her luggage. He moved to the bathroom. Toothbrush, toothpaste, hair spray, everything in place.

The manager came to the doorway to see what Duke was up to. Duke brushed right by him and spoke to Sullivan. "Everything looks fine. Let's get a car to watch the building and let us know when she shows up."

Sullivan and Duke sat in their car waiting for the backup. "No doubt in my mind her friend Cathy called her right after our visit," Duke said. "She sure as hell cleared out of the office fast. You think it was McCallister she saw in the park?"

Sullivan rubbed his face with both hands. "Who the hell knows anymore? But what would he be doing walking around in the park just after the police leave his place?"

"Maybe looking for his visitor, to beat him up some more," Duke suggested.

Sullivan groaned. "I thought you'd pretty much decided he'd already done the guy in, now you're telling me he's still alive. Make up your mind."

Duke settled back into his seat, frowning.

"Here's the backup," Sullivan said as headlights drew up behind them. "Get the guys up to speed and let's go home and get some dinner."

TWENTY-SIX

Daniel and Sylvia looked at the ugly headline together, then put the paper aside. They'd made many promises during the night; one was to take the next days, or months, one moment at a time. Neither wanted to lose the closeness they'd rediscovered.

"You aren't going into the office today, are you?" Sylvia asked.

"It would be too awkward for everyone. I can afford a day or two off."

At ten o'clock, as they finished breakfast, the doorbell rang.

"Dad's here," Sylvia said, as she came back into the kitchen, Tom Halliburton in tow.

Tom's handsome face was lined with concern. Daniel rose from his chair. Tom gripped Daniel's hand, then moved closer to give him a hug and a heavy slap on the back. "Damn, Danny. Hell of a mess."

Sylvia handed her father a cup of coffee.

Daniel anticipated one reason why Tom looked so harried. "The party's dumped me, haven't they?"

"Danny, I did all I could, but once it hit the papers, with all that innuendo about abandoning a

216

brother in need, even the possibility that you might be charged, they had no choice."

Daniel's face fell. He shook his head slowly. "I expected it, but it's still a shock to actually get the news." Sylvia came to his side, sliding her arm under his. "Who's it going to be?" he asked.

Halliburton answered unenthusiastically. "Paul Brigham."

"They think he can do the job?"

"Hell, Danny, we all know no one else can do the job. You were our ace. But I don't envy Brigham. He'll go down like a rocket. It'll put the party back a good eight, ten years."

Daniel looked down at the floor.

"Hell," Halliburton continued, flustered, "it's not your fault. Rotten luck." He looked back and forth between Sylvia and Daniel. Neither had anything to say. "Well, I'd better get along." He kissed Sylvia on the cheek, handed her his untouched coffee, and turned to Daniel. "You know where I am," he offered.

Mid-afternoon Daniel received a call from Detective Sullivan.

"We'd like to speak to your assistant, Miss Jones," he said, "but can't locate her. Would you have any ideas where she might be?"

Daniel could not believe she was not in the office at this crucial time. "Surely Rosie's not involved in this mess," he said, even as his mind made the connection between her and Roger that Levy had always suspected. He mentioned her family, who operated a ranch somewhere near the city, but Sullivan had already called there.

"Did you see Miss Jones on Saturday night?"

"No. I've told you about that night a dozen times." Sullivan didn't actually grunt into the phone, but Daniel could feel his suspicions running right through the line. As he replaced the receiver, he brushed a thin line of sweat from his brow. Why this sudden interest in Rosie? Did they have the photograph of him in her apartment building? He told Sylvia he was going into the office after all, but would not stay long.

Daniel found Cathy at her desk, bundled in a heavy sweater. Her eyes were sunken, her nose swollen and red.

"You don't look good. Should you be here?" he asked.

"I called, but Rosie wasn't here, so I thought I'd better come in."

"Do you know where she is?"

"There's a note addressed to you on your desk, in her handwriting."

Tucked under the corner of Daniel's desk blotter was a twice-folded piece of paper with his name written on the outside.

Daniel, please forgive my not giving you more notice, but I need a few days off. My mother is ill. I'll be in touch. Rosie.

Daniel read it again. According to Sullivan, she was not with her sick mother. He was about to place a call to Levy when a hesitant knock sounded on his door.

Cathy put her head in. "Can I talk to you?"

Besides the reddening puffiness from her cold, her face was twisted as though she were controlling tears. Daniel motioned her forward and she sat opposite him, immediately producing a tissue and wiping her nose.

"Oh, Mr. McCallister," she murmured without looking up, "I'm really worried about Rosie."

Daniel waited, impatient with her weepiness.

"Two detectives came to my house on Monday asking all kinds of questions. They badgered me about where I'd been Saturday night. It was awful." He was still looking at the top of her head and wished she would sit up. "Then they asked about my car. They'd seen it near your house. Rosie had borrowed it."

Daniel frowned, trying to understand. "Do you know why she would have been at my place Saturday night?"

Cathy pulled another tissue from her pocket and wiped at her eyes. Then she raised her head. "She thought you were getting ready to fire her. She wanted to talk to you in private."

"Fire her?" Daniel tried to sound surprised. "Why did she think that?"

"Not going on the cross-country trip. Your turning things over to Billy. She was feeling left out."

"What happened after the detectives questioned you?"

"I called Rosie immediately. She sounded really upset when I mentioned they had seen the car. She practically hung up on me. What's going on Mr. McCallister? Is Rosie in trouble?"

"I don't know. Will you excuse me? I need to call Mr. Levy."

Before Daniel could say anything Barry offered his condolences about the party's decision.

"I understand it," Daniel said. "We'll get past it. What I need to know is whether you will continue to represent me, on a personal basis."

"Daniel, I'll be with you until we're clear of this mess."

"It gets stickier," Daniel said, telling Levy about Sullivan's call. Barry immediately went back on the offensive, as Detective Sullivan had.

"You never mentioned a visit from Rosie."

"I never *had* a visit from Rosie. I had no idea she was anywhere near the house."

"We need to know what she was doing there. More important, did she see anything or anyone? You're sure you can't reach her?"

"She's apparently left the city for a few days."

The silence on the phone made Daniel's skin crawl. He knew what Levy was thinking; once again, Rosie seemed to be manipulating his life.

"I'll call Greenburg. If she was spotted in the area someone must have come forward. Maybe he'll throw us a crumb."

Within minutes Levy called back. "Greenburg was close-mouthed, but he admitted they have the license plate and a witness who saw someone similar in size to Rosie in the park, after the officers were at your house." Levy's voice became animated. "This is good news, Daniel; shifts the focus from you. Opens up possibilities."

"Such as?"

"Was she involved with Roger all along? Had they planned to rendezvous in the park after he left your place? Think hard, Daniel. We've got to find her."

Daniel sat quietly after Levy hung up. He didn't want to think of Rosie duping him, even though he'd given her every reason to do so.

TWENTY-SEVEN

Rosie put aside her paperback novel. She'd read the same page twice and still didn't know what it said. The elderly woman beside her was snoring comfortably, the smell of liverwurst pungent on her breath. The black night, rushing by outside, made her own reflection under the bus's reading light very clear. The short blonde wig was amazingly natural looking, but it still startled her. She rubbed the back of her neck and as her hand came down her emerald ring flashed in the light. "Damn," she said, taking it off immediately and putting it in the shiny plastic purse.

Life had been hell since Cathy's phone call on Monday. After leaving the office, she'd flown to Regina and stayed the night in a cheap hotel. Not wanting to travel in daylight, she waited until nighttime to catch the bus. She'd spent the day finding the wig and a few more clothes and now was well away from Regina. She planned to get off the bus in Winnipeg, spend a day or two and then head for Toronto.

She couldn't concentrate on her book because her mind kept wandering back to Saturday night. Why had she been so stupid as to go into that park?

She'd circled the neighborhood and was headed back to Daniel's house when she thought she saw him in the park. It was a quick look, but the man's size, the slope of his shoulders under the lamplight, and something about the way he moved, brought Daniel immediately to mind. Of course she was off balance and confused, having seen the police at his house. She remembered looking around the area before leaving her car, calling to him, then moving slowly into the park.

The grass became very wet, then springy, then mush, ruining her good shoes. She pushed to her left, the direction she thought Daniel had gone. Impenetrable black stretched between the sporadic spots of lamp light. She stopped to listen but only the roar of the river could be heard.

"Daniel," she called. "It's Rosie."

Another minute went by with no sound, no movement. Suddenly it seemed very spooky to be there all alone. She turned to go back to the car.

An arm came from behind a tree and grabbed her coat. The man jerked her toward him, into the shallow water. His face, in the scarce light, was monstrous. His hair and beard dripped. Blood ran from his forehead. His whole body shook, like someone demented. Her mouth gaped open in a frantic attempt to scream. A long dry rasping sound was all that came out. He held both her arms tightly at her side and pulled her so close she felt his breath on her face. His head moved as his eyes ranged over her.

"Rosie?" he said plaintively.

Her knees buckled; she went limp.

Blackness took her away for a few moments. She came back to consciousness, his arms wrapped fully around her. Her toes reached for the ground as he held her. Their mouths were almost touching. She tried to twist away.

"Rosie, it's okay," the man whispered. The stench of his breath almost choked her. "It's Roger. If you stop struggling, I'll let you stand."

She stared into his face and could see no resemblance, but he'd fooled her before. Stunned with relief that he wasn't a stranger bent on hurting her, she felt life returning to her limbs. "Put me down."

He allowed her to stand, and step back just a few inches, but still gripped her coat sleeves. Then he began to ramble, whining.

"You've got to help me, Rosie. I lost my glasses. I can't see. I fell off Daniel's rock wall into the river. You've got to help me, Rosie."

She shrugged out of his grasp and he let her go. She moved backward a few steps to slightly higher ground. The bottoms of her legs were soaked and freezing. He didn't follow, but stood, still in the swirling water, shivering violently. He clutched his hands over his chest.

"Please, Rosie," he begged. "Don't leave me. The police were shining their spotlight so I had to stay in the water. I'm freezing."

There was a long pause. Roger's moans blended with the river's voice.

"Were you at Daniel's house?" she demanded.

"Yes."

"Why were the police there?"

"I don't know, Rosie. They just came. Please, help me. I'm almost frozen. Just help me get home. I can't see." He reached out for her.

She smacked at his outstretched hand. "Why were the police there?" she shouted.

"I don't know." He wrapped his arms around his body as if to contain the violent shivering.

"Don't lie to me, Roger. I can see what you've done. You finally managed to suck Daniel into your creepy little fantasy. You called them, didn't you? Have you finally managed to ruin him?"

Roger let out a sob. "God, Rosie, no. Nothing like that."

Rosie gritted her teeth, her fright completely replaced by seething anger. She spit the words at him. "Why should I believe you? And why should I help you? I worked damned hard to get where I am and now you've screwed everything up!"

She stepped forward and lashed out at him, striking his shoulder. "Haven't you," she screamed, pummeling him with her fists.

Roger fell off balance and grabbed at her arm to steady himself. She realized she had the better of him. Murderous hatred clouded her vision. She put all her weight into the shove that sent him flailing backwards.

His arms spun as his feet were swept out from under him and he fell into the river. He was completely submerged for a moment. Then she saw him again, downstream, his outstretched form outlined by the moonlight. Rosie stood stock still as she watched him thrash around. One arm rose above the level of the water and his voice drifted back to her. "Rosie . . ." Then the water took him again.

Rosie turned as if to look out the dark window of the bus. But her gaze was inward. She had a moment's glimpse of a brazen young man at the rodeo, who thought she was beautiful, who was willing to keep her secret. She shivered.

There was no use trying the novel again, she couldn't remember anything about the story. The edge of a newspaper stuck out of the old woman's canvas bag which was planted between her boots. Rosie lifted it slowly, inch by inch, so as not wake her.

She'd read of Daniel's predicament, which gave her some solace. Her coming forward would definitely save him, but she had no doubt he would skate through it without her. Money and influence were everything in this world, and here she sat in cheap polyester slacks with the pleats sewn in.

She opened the paper as quietly as possible. After reading a few paragraphs about the new direction the investigation was taking, she let it crumple beneath her suddenly heavy arms.

Rosie sat immobile while her mind spun. She might as well turn around at the next stop; there would be no evading the police now. Her well-honed sense of self-preservation kicked in immediately. On the ride back she would have plenty of time to remember how she'd gone into the park, only to find that Roger waited there, not Daniel. She began to picture the way Roger had pulled her against him and tried to ravage her and how hard she had struggled, barely escaping his attack. Hadn't he been stalking her for years? Terrified, she had run from the park while his ugly threats rang in the air. Then, frightened that Roger would search her out, she'd gone into the office Monday morning to retrieve her personal things, and left the city.

Rosie retrieved the emerald ring from her handbag and put it on, admiring its beauty. She dragged the wig from her head and loosened her hair. Sitting up very straight she looked at herself in the window. Even without makeup it was a commanding face, and there were other Daniel McCallisters in the world.

TWENTY-EIGHT

Daniel pushed aside blueprints for an ice-skating rink, which McCallister Engineering was building for the city, to read the morning's mail. Just then the intercom buzzed.

"Yes?"

"Billy's here," Cathy said. "Have you got a minute?"

"Of course, send him in." Daniel realized he hadn't even said goodbye to Billy when his campaign collapsed. Billy had been a fervent Majority Party backer, and Daniel assumed he was still active in the trenches.

The young man entered, closing the door carefully behind him. He seemed almost frightened. "Hey, things can't be that bad in the Brigham camp," Daniel said. He reached across the desk to shake Billy's limp hand.

"May I sit down?"

Daniel motioned to the arm chair. "Certainly. What's the matter?"

Billy pulled an envelope from his jacket pocket and took out several strips of exposed film. He fanned them on the edge of the desk, pushing one particular strip toward Daniel.

228

He spoke very quietly. "I'm very embarrassed about this. This is the film with a picture of you at Rosie's apartment."

"What?" Daniel exclaimed. He stood and picked up the strip, holding it up to the light. All the rectangles were blank but one—the one showing him in the lobby. Shock was soon replaced by anger. "*You* took it?"

Billy seemed to flinch. "It's not what you think."

Daniel took a deep breath, waiting.

Billy rubbed his hand across his face. "You see, I felt something was going on between you and Rosie. Then, that night, when we three went to dinner, I was sure of it. I was afraid that if I had figured it out, others might as well. I followed you that night, to be sure. Then I remembered I had the camera in the car, and, well . . ." The last few words tumbled out quickly. "I took the picture to warn you off, to tell you to be careful."

"Why didn't you just come to me?" Daniel asked in frustration.

"I'm sorry. I just couldn't," Billy said. "I was in awe of you."

Daniel noted the past tense.

"I hope it didn't cause too much trouble," Billy muttered.

Daniel sat back down, his face hard. Too much trouble? He remembered alienating Rosie because of the picture. But if Rosie hadn't come looking for him that night, to clear the air, she wouldn't have found Roger in the park. Without that fact, he might still be under suspicion of murder. It could be the best favor anyone had ever done him. "No harm done," he said.

After Billy left, Daniel took a pair of scissors from his drawer and cut the film into fine pieces, dumping them in his wastebasket, then returned to the business on his desk.

He reached for the top envelope in the mail stack. It was not typed, but in handwriting, marked 'Personal,' with a return address he didn't recognize. A letter-size piece of paper was folded around a black-and-white photo—a very worn picture of a young woman. Puzzled, Daniel read the few words scrawled on the paper. "Thought you'd like to have this. Det. Jerry Sullivan."

Daniel turned the photo over and his breath caught. It was Maryanne Scott. His mother as a young woman, maybe a teenager. And Roger's mother. He studied the face for a long time. "I wish I had known you," he whispered. "I wish you had known me." In her smile he recognized his own— they shared a twist in the left corner of the mouth. Her eyes were still young and eager, looking kindly on a world that would turn on her. Finally, he opened his wallet and slipped Maryanne's likeness inside. This gentle woman had given birth to two sons, and a good life to one—he would be forever grateful to her for that.

ABOUT THE AUTHOR

Marlene Baird grew up in the Canadian city where *Murder Times Two* is set. She escaped those windswept, frigid winters by moving to Honolulu, then California, and now lives among the Arizona pines with her husband. After working as an airline hostess and a legal assistant, Marlene turned to her true love, writing. Three of her short stories have been published and she has won numerous awards in nationwide writing contests.

Printed in the United States
3713